MW00623240

Selected Praise for Jesse Ball

Autoportrait

"Slim but powerful . . . The collisions of severe, unvarnished facts start to build a larger idea about how we live—or how we fail to live fully . . . A brave book . . . There is strength in it, and cleverness and nearly unbearable honesty."   —*Los Angeles Times*

"Jesse Ball's *Autoportrait*, you might say, is all voice . . . Evocative and bright."   —*Chicago Tribune*

The Divers' Game

"Jesse Ball is a writer of formal mysteriousness and neon moral clarity . . . His language is spare, strange, and evocative . . . His themes are human savagery, often state-sanctioned, and human kindness, a thin thread of resistance."   —*The New Yorker*

"Jesse Ball levels a steely gaze at the very concept of humanity in this three-part novel that introduces the lower-class 'quads' and the rich 'pats,' who treat those below them with impunity. When a group of pats conceals the grisly fate of a young quad girl behind an elaborate festival, you may start to wonder just how different this dystopian world is from our own."

—*The Washington Post*

Census

"Ball's most personal and best to date . . . A point—about the beautiful varieties of perception, of experience—made without sentimentality, burns at the core of the book, and of much of Ball's work, which rails against the tedium of consensus, the cruelty of conformity." —*The New York Times*

"*Census* is a vital testament to selfless love; a psalm to commonplace miracles; and a mysterious, evolving metaphor. So kind, it aches."

—David Mitchell, author of *Cloud Atlas*

"If there's a refrain running through Ball's large body of work, it's that compassion, kindness and empathy trump rules and authority of any kind . . . This damning but achingly tender novel holds open a space for human redemption, never mind that we have built our systems against it."

—*Los Angeles Times*

How to Set a Fire and Why

"The most remarkable achievement of this novel is its narrative voice . . . Sometimes, you hear the ghost of Kazuo Ishiguro's flat, chilly style. At other times . . . Borges-like parable cross-pollinates with Margaret Atwood–style dystopia."   —*The Boston Globe*

"Extremely well done: swift, sharp-tongued and enlivened by cockeyed humor."   —*The Wall Street Journal*

"A rare and startling work. Days after I read it, I find that I can't stop thinking about it, and what I've realized is that this is a book I will not forget. This is a harrowing, subtle, and absolutely electrifying novel."

—Emily St. John Mandel,
bestselling author of *Station Eleven*

Silence Once Begun

"Absorbing, finely wrought . . . A piercing tragedy . . . that combines subtlety and simplicity in such a way that it causes a reader to go carefully, not wanting to miss a word. " —Helen Oyeyemi,
The New York Times Book Review

"Ball enriches his metafictional restlessness with [a] humane curiosity . . . The language seems aware of the charged space around it, as if one were praying aloud in a darkened, empty church. His characters speak at once lucidly and uncannily; words have become strangely heavy."
—James Wood, *The New Yorker*

"Beginning as a work of seeming reportage, *Silence Once Begun* transforms into a graceful and multifaceted fable on the nature of truth and identity."
—Sam Sacks, *The Wall Street Journal*

THE REPEAT ROOM

ALSO BY JESSE BALL

Autoportrait
The Children VI
The Divers' Game
Census
The Way Through Doors
Samedi the Deafness
The Curfew
The Lesson
Silence Once Begun
A Cure for Suicide
How to Set a Fire and Why
March Book
The Village on Horseback
Fool Book
Vera & Linus
Og svo kom nottin
Deaths of Henry King
Notes on My Dunce Cap
Sleep, Death's Brother

AT ROOM THE REPEAT ROOM THE REI
AT ROOM THE REPEAT ROOM THE REI
AT ROOM THE REPEAT ROOM THE REI
AT ROOM THE REPEAT ROOM THE REI
AT ROOM THE REPEAT ROOM THE REI
AT ROOM THE REPEAT ROOM THE REI
AT ROOM THE REPEAT ROOM THE REI
AT ROOM THE REPEAT ROOM THE REI
AT ROOM THE REPEAT ROOM THE REI
AT ROOM THE REPEAT ROOM THE REI
AT ROOM THE REPEAT ROOM THE REI
AT ROOM THE REPEAT ROOM THE REI
AT ROOM THE REPEAT ROOM THE REI
AT ROOM THE REPEAT ROOM THE REI
AT ROOM THE REPEAT ROOM THE REI
AT ROOM THE REPEAT ROOM THE REI
AT ROOM THE REPEAT ROOM THE REI
AT ROOM THE REPEAT ROOM THE REI

THE REPEAT ROOM

A NOVEL

JESSE BALL

CATAPULT   NEW YORK

Copyright © 2024 by Jesse Ball

First Catapult edition: 2024

ISBN: 978-1-64622-140-0

Library of Congress Control Number: 2024939484

Jacket design and illustration by Sara Wood
Book design by Wah-Ming Chang

Catapult
New York, NY
books.catapult.co

Printed in the United States of America
1 3 5 7 9 10 8 6 4 2

THE REPEAT ROOM

There was a long counter in the diner. The lights were on, but there wasn't much. It was light for someplace smaller than that, maybe the light from the dash of an old car. It would have to do. It was a small diner, really just the counter, and the counter was empty but for a man and a woman. The man sat and before him was a grayish envelope. He was not fifty, but not forty either. His shoulders were solid. His face looked abused, broken. His hair was badly cut, and his chalk eyes looked where he pointed them. Right then he was looking at the counter, at the envelope, not at the woman in front of him. She had just finished saying something.

She was somewhere between twenty and forty, with a face and body like a photograph of a waitress. On her neck in serif it said *Carlos*. Maybe it said *forever*, too. Her weight was on one foot or the other. What she said then was:

"Not that you should listen to me. I don't care. Just as a courtesy I'm telling you. That bell goes off means you got to be over there. People who take their time, they probably wish they hadn't. I've worked here awhile. Take it for what it's worth."

The man looked over his shoulder out the window. The building opposite had a massive entranceway funneling down to a tiny single bronze door. Beside it was a guard booth. The building was a courthouse. It was an edifice of stone, something like a pyramid. In monumental letters was written: COURT 5. Someone was walking up the steps, infinitely small in that place, scarcely human.

"They ask you to come down, I guess they can wait their turn too," he said. "And anyway, it's not like you've been inside there." His voice was low and raspy. "Maybe it's a picnic."

"Suit yourself. What'll you have?"

He pointed to a menu inset in the counter. The waitress turned, went to a window in the wall, and shouted through it,

"Number six."

She pressed a button in the wall and coffee came out of a spigot into a cup she was holding. The next part of her dance was she put it in front of him and she looked at him and she looked through him.

"Service."

The man could see through the window to the kitchen. A face had appeared there, a ruddy-looking cook, fat and dirty, a short-order cook. He put a plate on the partition and turned away. The cook and the kitchen flickered for a second and there was just a wall there with a slot. Then it was there again and the cloth of the cook's linen-clad back was moving out of frame.

The waitress nodded to her customer.

"I used to ask people who they see in the hologram. For me it's my mom. No kidding. Twenty years dead but there she is. People say it's a man, it's a woman, one guy saw his brother. You remember when they put these in? People couldn't believe their luck. Now it's just garbage looking at garbage."

"Must get lonely in here," said the man. "No one to talk to."

"That's right," she said, and gave him his plate.

Her hands played with the waitress pad, turning it over and over. It wasn't even paper. It was just a block that looked like a waitress pad. You could see from her fingers she'd had a hard time. Fingers like that.

She was talking, mostly to herself, but she'd look up from time to time, like a child checking to see if it was asleep yet.

"I never envy the bastards who get the call. Pardon me, you're one of them, but it's the truth. I hope to God I never get that envelope in the mail. Me, I'm known to screw up anything and if I had to be a juror, well, I'd never make the cut. I mean if you knew you got to see it, got to see the room, well, maybe it's worth it. Everyone's curious about the repeat room. But there's no guarantee. I mean it's the opposite. And that's the thing, huh. Mess up in there, end up ranked down. There you were doing nothing, just trying to get by. Never knew you looked so much like a rat, did you?"

The man did something like a smile.

"I mean, I'm curious," she said. "Surely I am. I want to look inside somebody's head. But I'd be afraid too. I've heard people die doing it, time to time. You heard that?"

He put some money on the counter, picked up the envelope, inclined his head, and went out the door.

"You look like a nice type," she called after him. "Don't let 'em turn you around."

The man stood in a room. He was in a line. Others were behind him. He had been at the end of it, but now he had come to the front. The paint of the walls was itself the room's light source and it was too bright for human eyes. The man squinted his and looked up at the glass. A woman was looking down. The space between them was a barrier, but there were metal slats. Whether he was hearing her or hearing her voice reproduced no one could tell. Still she spoke and he heard. She was wearing some kind of cloth helmet that covered her hair.

"State your name, occupation, age, place of birth."

"Abel Cotter. Heavy-machine operator. Forty-six. Born Seaport District."

"Put your hand in the box."

A metal flap flipped up. It was somewhere he could put his hand. He did. Something locked over his hand; it was stuck. "Don't struggle. Just wait."

A clicking noise came through the intercom.

"Not really a heavy-machine operator, are you,"

said the woman. "More of a garbageman. Says here you're a garbageman."

The people in line behind him shifted uneasily. "It's a machine," he said, head down.

"Around here we want the truth. You can go to the next room. Show 'em your number."

As she spoke a noise of hydraulics releasing came out of the hole and with it his hand. He rubbed at it. There were black symbols there like numerals. A door opened in the wall.

He went through it, and the person behind him took his place.

A lamp flickered on and off in the ceiling. Abel sat on a long bench. Ten or twenty people were beside him. The same opposite, just a few feet away. A girl with short hair wearing a tight sweater and not much else. Another girl wearing a cast on her arm. The man beside him stank of liquor, old liquor. A woman with dark glasses and a birthmark elbowed him as she sat. There really wasn't any space. It was like people say: a submarine, being on a submarine. Like that. Someone in the line was talking to somebody else, saying,

"They want you to get used to each other."

"I don't think that's it."

"Yeah, they want you to get used to each other. It's a competition."

"It's not a competition."

"But you can sure fuck it up."

"Nobody knows that."

Abel went with others into a room with lockers. There they changed out of their clothes and into other clothing, light-yellow-colored robes like hospital gowns, but more substantial. Some of the bodies he looked at in the room were soft and useless, others muscular. Some were male, some female. Everyone had to change in front of everyone else. The place was so squat and pitiless, so endless, repetitive, fluorescent. There was nothing sexual to be found there.

"Did you know it would be like this?" an old woman asked the girl next to her. The girl was naked, trying to put on the unirobe. She looked like a recruit.

She wasn't bothered by anyone's eyes.

"It's not something to know," she said. "You just put your robe on."

The old woman asked if anybody knew how long it was going to take. Someone told her to shut her mouth, shithead. Someone else told them, shut your mouth. Nobody was listening to anybody else, not really. The ceiling of the locker room was low. None of the lockers had locks, but there were cameras on the walls.

"You put your clothes somewhere. You come back later and get them. It's easy." That's what the recruit told the old shithead.

Abel leaned against the wall a minute and closed his eyes. People were standing there near him, but he was inconsequential to himself, empty.

"The cool type, huh? Waiting it out? I get it. Don't worry, I get it. Probably the best bet."

A short low-slung man was crouched on his heels. Boyish and somehow prematurely old. His yellow garment touched the ground like a woman's dress. He wiped his nose roughly, like he was helping someone else do it. He winked at Abel.

A bell rang. Silence. It rang again.

"I guess that's the signal. We keep going deeper. Aren't you curious?" Abel met the man's eyes. What was there was just spilloff.

They went down a hallway, in line like children, some stumbling here and there, unused to such order. The walls were nondescript. There was no signage. The floor was an oddly soft plastic, green like putty. The foot didn't sink into it, but the tromping of feet made no report. After ten minutes they came to a door which the official unlocked. They'd watched her walk the whole way but she'd shown nothing, given no details. The task was to walk them in the hallway. When she was doing it, she was the one walking them in the hallway. There wasn't anything else there. This was the new way for people to be, the new era. The balsa wood can be used once, then it breaks.

"Find a place wherever you can."

Room A was enormous and it was full of people dressed like they were dressed, like mental patients, lounging like full-time losers on the hard benches. The newcomers were no different, except they hadn't found seats. They were later than the others, who must have come on time, or early, or even days before. It was a real gathering. No one was missing. Every sort of person was there. It had the cheap expectation of a carnival tent. Abel looked for somewhere to sit and saw it on the far side. He went there. A man with a cane was taking up two or three spots. Abel made him take up two, and sat in his own space, quietly, looking down at the marks on his hand.

The old man looked at him from time to time. He had thick white hair and heavy glasses under which his face shook without warning. He would take his glasses off and then put them back on again, God knows why.

"Do you think it'll be long?"

"I don't know."

"Who is going to speak to us?"

Avoiding the question, Abel looked at his robe. Then he looked at the robes the others were wearing. Each of the robes had a number on it.

"Be careful," the old man told him. "Whole thing's a trick to get you to confess to something. Or to get you to do something you shouldn't."

"Pshaw," said a stocky woman on the other side. "The only ones getting it are the ones who've got it coming." Her hands were kneading her knees and her knees stuck out. The skin there was fibrous and peeling.

The old man inclined his head in disagreement.

A flat tone, unpleasant by design, loudened and filled the space until all speech ceased. A projection appeared on the wall and people turned to face it. The visage there was another official's, not particularly male or female, but the voice was deep.

"This is the jury. You have been selected at random in order to be what you are now, a jury. The next three days, today, tomorrow, and the next day, are the jury selection, training, and trial, a selection from the pool of candidates, from the group here assembled. As you perhaps have heard, we will train you and in training you we will winnow you down until there is only one left. Everyone else will be removed, having demonstrated their unfitness. Only one person will be left, one fit person. That person will be the jury for the case in question. It will be this single opinion that makes the statement of life or death. You may be a coward. This has been taken into account. Do not try to evade the duty for which you are a candidate. The consequences for such cowardly behavior are severe. From now on all errors, misbehaviors, back talk, will be penalized under code 4429-762. This is not your regular life. Have a care."

The projection blinked out, leaving just the warning behind.

A moment later the tone again. Then another projection.

What they saw was a jail cell and in it a man sitting on a stool. He looked up at the camera and said nothing. He was young, possibly still a teenager. He was several days unshaven and his eyes were ringed with sleep. In the cell you couldn't see how large he was. He could have been any size.

"This is the person for whom you are here. From time to time we will show you his image to acquaint you with your task.

"What do you think he did?"

The old man was right by his elbow. "What do you think?"

"I don't know."

"Must have been something bad." The old man laughed.

"Must have been pretty bad to get the death sentence, eh? Still, I'd like to know. Kid like that, looks like a fuck-off. Dirty like that, like he was."

"Looks like they make him sit in that cell, maybe it's not his fault he's dirty."

"Oh, he's dirty all right," said the stocky woman. "I know hundreds just like him. That's the kind of neighborhood I live in."

"It's not supposed to matter what he did, is it? That's not the job," said Abel.

"That's right," said the old man, "not supposed to, but it does matter. It matters, doesn't it?"

"That's the point," said Abel slowly. "That's the whole thing. It's about what you will do, not what you did."

"Don't bother talking to him," the woman told Abel. "He's irrelevant."

"I don't have to put up with this," said the old man, standing up.

There was no place for him to go, though, so all he could do was sit down again.

"See, like I said. Irrelevant. Your time is done."

The woman coughed into her hand. It sounded like part of her lung had come loose, but no one looked at her.

Now they sat at partitioned desks facing blocky screens like concave lamps. Abel wore thick headphones and stared into the centermost point, where the light converged. Stare at the monitor. Stare at the monitor. Stare at the monitor. Be ready and speak. A small green sphere appeared. He said that. A flame like a candle but no candle. He said that. Something bony, an ankle, but without a foot or leg. A moment passed. It flickered away. A swishing tail, a cat's tail appeared, followed by a trombone, a contour map, a plate of spaghetti, a face biting its lip. He said what these were, rapidly, quietly. There was a meter on the wall of the partition. When he would answer quickly it would rise. When he would slow down it would fall. He sped up. Sock puppet. Battery pack. Musical instrument, no, dulcimer. Cartoon mouse. Teacup. Rosebush. Helicopter. The meter flashed at the top. Now someone was behind him, an official, helping him to his feet.

He removed the headphones and followed the man out of the room, past dozens of desks. The muttering was loud taken together. Names of things without urgency said urgently, pulped into incoherence against what else was said, where the else was just what happened to be said. It wasn't even clear what you were supposed to say. They were all just saying what they saw.

The attendant walked ahead of him with a swaying step. Her shirt and pants were carefully fitted, but institutional. Her hair was in many small braids. She had the fragility of youth, but her face was serious, like someone who had just been told a secret. The attendant took him down three or four hallways to a door marked Examinations.

"I'm Marna," she said. "Sometimes I'll be dealing with your case."

"Abel."

"No, no, no." She laughed.

She reached out and touched the number on his arm. "This is who you are for our purposes. No names, please."

She depressed a metal square on the wall. The door opened. Inside, three officials were sitting facing a single chair.

"Please sit."

The room was faced on one side with a mirror. Abel watched himself, watched the broken-down man sit in a plastic chair like he was told to.

"Why do you think this is the way it's done?"

He said he didn't know.

"Okay, smart guy. Then what do you think it is? What is the way it's done?"

He said so far it didn't make sense.

"What have you been told about it? What have you heard?"

He said he knew it was like a movie. Like you watched a movie, but it was a person who didn't know they were acting. They were having their real life to them.

"It is a person who doesn't know they are acting. They are in a special chamber, the room. This repeat room can be made to expose them to whatever experience we like. What they bring is themselves and how they are. We are judging that, we as a society.

The juror is the agent of that judgment, the judger, the judge. A scenario is chosen, matched to what we know of them and what they've done. You may have heard of some of the scenarios. Have you heard of them?"

He said he had heard of one or two. There was one with a lost cat.

"The lost cat scenario. That one has seized the public imagination."

A different official interjected, "It's amusing, because it's so rarely seen, but it's the one that . . ."

"Yes, it's the one people think of."

"Do you remember what it was like before? You were educated thirty to forty years ago. You were taught about the primitive court system. Are you in favor of that system? Many people your age think they are. They think that because they haven't thought about it. Are you?"

He said people can do what they like. His opinion so far hadn't mattered.

"But if it did?"

He looked at the officials for the first time. One was a redheaded man whose face beneath the eyes was covered with a thick beard like straw. The next was a girl, or practically so. She couldn't have been more than eighteen years old. Still, it had been her doing the talking. The third was a bald man with a scar on his lip, something surgical or a knife injury. His eyes were very large and seemed kind. Where the others were upright he was bent, inclining as if in offering. He was farthest away.

"Well, the other way didn't work so well," said Abel cautiously.

The official laughed.

"Do you understand the difference between the systems?"

Abel inspected his feet. His toenails needed cutting, just like every other time he'd looked at them.

"It's useless," said the bearded man. "Look at his dossier. He's not suited."

"Candidate," said the girl. "State the difference if you understand it between the two systems."

"One punishes. The other looks forward."

"So you've seen the billboards," she said wryly. "You don't always just look at your feet."

He sat in a room by himself. It was a large room with many chairs. After a while someone came in and sat down. He didn't look at them. They didn't look at him. Another came. Then another. More came, none looking at the others. Soon there were many there, none of whom could say who they were sitting near. None of them wanted to look and none did. They were all looking at the air a foot in front of their faces. Not past that. When the seats were all full, the lights came up in the front. As one, the audience shifted and became still.

A man with a face like an old debt came out under the lights. He looked like he was about to speak. A woman followed him out, tapped him on the shoulder, whispered something. They argued briefly. He left the stage. The woman bowed and began.

"That was just a mix-up," she said. "That's the kind of thing happens when two people try to be in the same place at the same time. Kind of the problem we got here, only it's a thousand people trying to fit into one pair of pants. Not like you came of your own free will. Good citizens."

She shook her head.

"Anyway, you got me here now, so let's start."

Once she started talking, her voice was very loud, louder than anyone would expect. When she turned away and turned back, you felt it, even at a distance. Where she stood the ceiling was low. It was like she was standing in a box. There was something theatrical about it, the way the space framed her. She seemed perfectly suited to it. The cuff of one of her sleeves was rolled up, but it revealed nothing. She was describing the execution process. Her mode of speaking was expansive.

"Jurisprudence should not have to do with the past. It is, like education, a promise of a future, a kind of future. The future is what?"

She gazed into the audience.

"It is what we bring to it together. Therefore the question posed is: Who are we? Who gets to be a part of this group, we? Therefore the penalty of failing to appear to be fit is to be removed from the group. That is why the penalty is execution. It is not a matter of good and evil. It is a practical matter. When the cat scratches your sofa, you must question whether it is the right cat for you. Wrong cats do not stay in the house for long."

She walked up the aisle and stood at the back of the audience. The heads did not follow her. They stared straight ahead, waiting for her to continue.

"I am an explainer. You are know-nothings. Ask me things and I'll explain them. Are there any questions?"

"How is it done?"

"How is it done."

She repeated the question so everyone could hear it, but without emphasis, and walked back to the front of the room.

"Do you know ways it used to be done? Say them."

People began to speak up like it was a classroom. Not knowing how they could please anyone, they showed their infallible immaturity and leapt at the chance to distinguish themselves.

"Drowning." "Hanging." "Electrocution." "Injection." "Guillotine." "Axe."

"Shooting squad."

"Made to walk in the desert."

"They'd push you from a cliff."

"Cut your throat."

"Starve you."

She nodded at each entry, listening carefully. When she'd heard enough she raised one hand:

"Some of these are messy. Others simply work badly, inefficiently. People don't die the way they should, and it has to be done again. Generally, we find, executions were handled better long ago. The more people think people have value, the worse they are at killing them. This is true of course only in this case. In war we go on year by year, better and better at it. Yes?"

A woman with a shaved head and glasses had her hand raised. "Which one is used now?"

"Isn't it interesting that no one here knows? For some reason, you aren't told that, the public. But you will be told now, for the reason that you should imagine it happening to the man you saw earlier today. You should imagine it in order to know what it is to take your job seriously. Does this make sense?"

Some heads nodded. Others stayed curiously poised.

"Let's look at him now. Let's take a look at him again."

A projection blinked on behind her. The young man in the prison cell was there in the room with them. It was like he could see them there. He stood up and moved towards them, but there was only a few feet he could go. One of his eyes was a little red, and the second-to-last button on his shirt hadn't been fastened. There was an air about him—somehow all of who he was hadn't been poured into his container. It was a person there, for sure, but visibly shallow. Yet his eyes were large and to look in the room was to look at them. He turned his thin back and the image winked out.

"The method is that the surplus person is put in a concrete room with a sealed door. After a little while the breathable air is removed from the room. Then biological death occurs. This process has no flaws and does not suffer from any of the difficulties of the old processes. It works one hundred percent of the time and costs the taxpayer almost nothing. Try all they like, the lungs learn they have no job to do."

She made a little bow at the shoulders.

"The new society is not pretty. It just does what it can to not be false and to permit no falseness. Can you picture it? Can you try? Picture that boy in a concrete room, a kind of killing jar, yes? Feel your lungs now. Put your hands on your chest, please. Do that now."

Everyone put their hands on their chest.

"Feel your lungs and how they rise and fall. Now

hold your breath. Hold it as long as you can. Hold it until you can hold it no longer and your eyes swim in points of light. This is how you will kill him, if you choose to.

"Next question," the woman called. "Don't be shy. It's not like we're watching your every move, waiting for a mistake . . ."

She laughed in spite of herself at that.

From behind Abel, a feeble voice said something. People turned.

"Say it again."

Someone else spoke up, one person doing someone else a favor like you sometimes hear of.

"She said, is it dangerous?"

"Is what dangerous?"

The feeble one told the other one what was dangerous and the other one asked, "They say jurors die with that helmet on. Is it so?"

The woman at the front bit her lip a little and scratched her face with one finger.

"The question, so everyone can hear it, is: Do jurors die? The question was asked with regard to some of the equipment used in the process, that being a helmet that the juror wears when viewing the contents of the repeat room. Evidently some of you know more than others about this. We'll try to get you all onto the same page, as it were. I will answer this question now."

She pulled a stool out and sat.

"The repeat room is a phenomenon, a process, that has been in use for ten years. Ten years. It's a long time. At the outset, its use was not perfected as it is now. There were cases at first where jurors could not bear the stresses of the task. There were deaths. But over the years there have been developments, and you need not fear for your safety."

There were a bunch of questions then. People wanting to know what the developments were.

"Okay, all right, quiet now. One was pharmaceutical. There are medicines that blunt the ill effects. Another was behavior modification. You have some, let's call them, interactions, and the interactions put you in a frame of mind that's helpful. Finally, we have gotten better at finding people who can bear the stress, and also at identifying those who cannot. In any case, it is a part of life in this civil society, and no one has to do it twice."

"When was the last death?" a man in the front row asked.

"There have been no deaths since the second year of institution. There really is nothing to fear anymore."

"But what about sickness?"

"What if we're allergic to the medicine?"

"What if we decide we can't do it, just can't? Not me, I mean, but, just someone?"

"Where is the prisoner now? Is he in this building behind one of these doors?"

The woman held her hand up for silence.

"I think we may have gone through enough questions for now. Those of you who are here tomorrow will have the opportunity to ask more. For now let me leave you with this thought: If someone's life is at issue, isn't it a grave enough thing for a juror to take a risk herself to see if that life can be saved?"

Behind Abel, someone muttered, "You don't save lives here, you take 'em . . ."

The speaker went to the door and opened it.

"I used to joke that if you were a good enough bunch, you wouldn't have to go right now to be cleaned, but people didn't like the joke. Reason is you're going to have to be cleaned no matter what you do. Into the hallway, please, one at a time."

The same attendant, Marna, took Abel Cotter and the others to a hallway lined on both sides with shallow closets. On the glass partition it read again and again frontways and backwards H Y G I E N E . E N E I G Y H . H Y G I E N E . E N E I G Y H all the way down.

Over the loudspeaker, a message came.

"Mandatory cleaning. Remove your garment and step inside."

Abel looked at the closet, shook his head almost unconsciously, and looked back at the attendant. She pointed to the closet.

"I'm sorry. You have to comply. Remove your garment and step inside."

The closet was narrow and the door was heavy. It wasn't somewhere anyone wanted to go. He hung his garment on a peg, took a breath, got in, and the door shut. He opened his mouth as if to scream, but no noise came out. Immediately it started getting hotter. It became hotter and hotter, hotter and hotter and hotter and hotter. Sweat formed on his back and chest and forehead, and he shook a little, like a worried animal. It felt like a trick. The door was an inch from his face. A horrific deep-frequency tone began, a tone so low he could hardly hear it. It shook his legs and chest. It shook his bowels. The noise grew worse and worse. It was all he could do to stand, and as he stood, he shat and pissed on his legs and feet. Almost immediately, as if in answer, the temperature began to decrease. Water sprayed over him from every direction. It was cold, very cold, then it became hot again, hotter and hotter. Finally there was just a mist that turned to nothing then dryness. The dryness increased until he could feel his skin like paper. The door to the outside opened and the attendant was watching him. She was handing out garments as people skulked out into the hall. She handed him a garment. This one was yellow too. It was the same as the one he'd worn before, but it was not that one. He put it on and followed her. His knotted shoulders made bunches in the cloth. His sallow, ill-treated neck rose from the hemmed neck hole to where his head rode in the air above his shoulders, its weight settling always implacably down. Like a puppet when one looks at it, he was for that moment more real than the things around him. Equally laughably obvious: he couldn't possibly be the center of anything and neither can you.

They were waiting for the food to be served. Maybe a third of them were left. At lunch they'd taken up the whole room. Now they sat in patchy bunches, with here and there a singleton. The thing is, people who are unqualified are always disqualifying themselves. That's what it means to be unqualified. Helplessly, you demonstrate who you are.

A large man with the face of a gin-drinker was relating a story.

"The cat is some kind of doctor. I mean, it's a cat, but they're all animals, so essentially that means they're all people. They're not animals at all, right? The cat's on a train and the lady, the conductor, who's a rabbit, she says, 'Is there a doctor in the house?' at which point . . ."

"But it's an opera?"

"It's an opera, yeah, an opera. I mean, they're singing this stuff. And the cat says, 'I'm a doctor.' And the one who's all fucked up, it's a bird, okay, and its wing is just hanging down, really badly broken, the bird, you can tell the bird doesn't trust the cat. The cat's like, 'Come into this compartment with me.' But the bird's stressed. Bad off as the bird is, it doesn't want to go. It just kind of looks at its feet and says, 'What kind of doctor?' and the rabbit laughs."

"The rabbit laughs?"

"Why does the rabbit laugh?"

"How come it laughs?"

Abel looked at the woman next to him. She saw him looking; their eyes met. "Why'd the rabbit laugh?"

"It's a joke," said Abel. "An old joke."

"But why."

"I don't know."

"Come on, you know. Tell me."

Abel shrugged.

"I guess a doctor that's a cat just, just eats the bird, right. He eats it."

The bellicose man was still talking. People were laughing at the punch line, whatever it was. They wanted him to keep going. Tell us more, things like that.

The food arrived on pale plastic trays. It was like

what you get when you fly somewhere, or when you've had a surgery.

"We did tests in pairs. Did you?" the woman asked. She was small, with blond hair like a doll and painted-on eyes.

"That was earlier?"

"Yeah, earlier."

"Yeah, I did that."

"The guy with me, he messed it up. He lied. I thought you'd get at least a chance, but he was just— sanctioned. It's a felony. They moved him to detention. He started crying."

"What's there to lie for?"

"I don't know, I didn't lie."

"What did you say if you didn't lie?"

"They asked if we'd ever committed any crimes. I said I didn't because I didn't. But he maybe did and he said he didn't."

"But if he said he did . . ."

"Yeah, that wouldn't have worked either. What'd they ask you?"

A woman opposite, with short thick black hair and a wide face, was leaning over the table. She'd said something.

"What?"

"I said, what are you talking about? You, him, talking. What about?"

"I'm Joan," said the one next to him.

"Lisette."

Abel said his name and looked at Joan. "You want to know what they asked me?"

"Yeah."

He thought about it.

Lisette spoke up in the meantime.

"I was there right next to, right next to Abel. I can tell you if he doesn't want to. They asked him why he couldn't get promoted even though he worked the same job for years. He's a garbageman. Then they asked, what did they ask next?"

She drummed her finger on the table.

"Oh, yeah, they asked how it felt to have bosses who were practically children. Not so nice, these people, what do you think? They asked why he never visited his mother in the home."

She paused.

"Apparently he never goes to visit his mother in the home." Joan turned her face to Abel.

"What did you say then?"

"I just said whatever came out."

"Whatever came out. That's good," said Lisette. "Someone like you doesn't know what he's doing, and then suddenly he knows what he's doing. That's good. Me, I've got some experience with this. I'm an arbitrator."

"I'm a student," said Joan.

"What kind of student?"

"Well, I was. I got kicked out of the school. Non-payment. Now I work at a grocery store. But I studied art. Drawing."

"Drawing," said Lisette, "that's a laugh. Who draws anymore? If I want a picture of a diver or a musket or an elephant riding a canary, I just ask the telescreen and there it is. If I want to adjust it, I adjust it. Who draws? Why would you do that?"

She made a kind of huffing sound. She was a heck of a talker.

"Anyway," she continued, "that shower was really something, wasn't it?"

A man on the other side agreed that it was something.

"I don't want to go into it," continued Lisette. "But that's not my usual day-to-day, a shower like that. I don't know what yours were like, but . . . I'll be glad if that never happens again. Matter of fact, I'd like a written apology. Guess I won't get one."

Whenever she said anything, she looked around to see how it had gone. But nobody was looking.

Abel said something to Joan, and from above the room looked appallingly bare, like an empty sandbox. The lights were the kind that kept people cheerful, for the kind of people who have trouble being cheerful.

"It wasn't really non-payment," Joan whispered to Abel. She put her hand on his arm and looked over his shoulder, away behind him as she spoke. They were in the hall now, waiting in line.

"No?"

"No. I didn't pass one examination and that's it. It's pretty strict."

He looked straight ahead, but his expression softened.

"And that's the only thing you wanted to be? An artist?"

"Yeah, since I was a kid."

"I'm sorry."

"You want to know something funny?"

"Yeah, sure."

"Well, I kind of liked that shower. It was like, what do they call those things, you get in a little wooden box and there's a stove in it . . ."

"A sauna?"

"Yeah, it was like a sauna. After you go through something like that, what's there to be ashamed of? I mean, I'm standing here and you're standing here, and we're just an hour or so past the time when we shat ourselves and we both know it."

He laughed at that. She did too, and when she laughed, you could see all her crooked teeth. It was the kind of thing that makes you trust someone.

"You still draw?"

"Sometimes."

Abel shook his head very slightly, pointlessly, a gesture without discernible meaning. He seemed like he was about to say something and then didn't. Then he did.

"When I was a kid, there was an artist lived on my street. I was just a boy then, I went into his house once for a glass of water. It was pretty, well, creepy. The things in there, I mean."

"Yeah, you're not supposed to know how to feel about art. That's how you know."

"How do you know what?"

"That's what they taught us in art school: that's how you know it's art."

The line started to move.

"Hey," said Joan, "hey."

"Yeah?"

"Most of these people are shits. I've talked to them a little. They're shits. But I hope it's you or me who gets it, who gets through to the end. I really want to see it. I want to see inside someone's fucking brain. I've been waiting my whole life for that."

Abel started to speak, but his voice was lost in the sound of arms, legs, sleeves, surfaces, hurry. Maybe he gave up, and nothing came out.

The line of them walking there: they looked like something out of Goya. It must have been the draping, and all the faces in harsh focus. Abel looked over his shoulder at the man behind him, not a fat man, not a young man, not strong, not sharp, just nothing, just a person flattened into the shape of a so-called person, but his life was in his face. That's how afraid he was of being seen.

"Stand over there."

This room was a small partition from a larger room. It was dark. On the floor by the window was a reflective line. Abel stood on it.

"I'm Ella. You remember me, I'm sure."

The official was the young woman from his examination. She stood by his side, also on the line. There wasn't much room there.

She wore an outfit that said somehow her status was high. Someone like Abel had never had clothes like that. And she was easy in them. They didn't mean anything to her, that's what it looked like. It was the new world, young people without a care, and when you pressed them on something, they had all the answers. Where did they get the script? Maybe they were right. And everyone old was just dying in a line, just waiting their turn to grab at something with a useless arm and collapse. You feel young but you're waiting, and young but you're waiting, and then, it's over, you're old, but it never began, the thing you were waiting for. When did it begin? How could it already be over?

"Just wait," she said. "The lights will go on. Don't speak. They can't hear us, but don't speak anyway. This is a place for listening."

After a minute, the lights went on. They were looking into a kind of interrogation room. Abel recognized it as a room he had been in earlier. A man was sitting in a chair. Three people faced him. They began to ask questions and the man tried to answer.

"Watch how he squirms in the chair. Do you see it?"

Abel nodded.

"Do you see how his chair is angled? It's impossible to sit properly in it. That puts him at an immediate disadvantage. Do you see how the lights in the ceiling are all angled so there is more light on him than on the interrogators?"

"Why?" said Abel softly.

"To find out who people are, to understand them, you have to defeat them. Why is that, do you think?"

"I don't know."

"It's because when they're defeated they have nothing left."

The man in the room was apologizing for being tired. Somehow this was the wrong thing to say, and the tenor of things got worse. They asked him to go and face the wall and he did so. He went to the mirror and stood. His face was very close to Abel's, but the man could only see himself. Abel stood there and looked at the man looking at himself helplessly. Abel's helplessness in watching the man who could do nothing either for himself or anyone else, it was not profound. It was elementally partial, intrinsically insufficient to be anything at all.

"If you think you know what you're doing," the official told Abel, "then you don't know what you're doing. You are here to learn how to see what people are. Look at him. He is one step from killing himself. That's because here he steps partway out of his life. Stepping out of it, he questions it. He can find nothing good in himself, or in others. Do you see that in his face?"

Abel closed his eyes for a moment and opened them again.

"Do you see how this man is unfit to be a juror? You want to hear something shocking. He came in here with a 4T designation."

She laughed.

"That won't last. Come with me."

Abel followed the woman out of the room and into another room. This one had a screen on the wall. The lights dimmed and the screen burst into being. They were looking at the interrogation room, the same one. But it was Abel in the room, in the chair, and officials were speaking to him. There was no sound.

"I want you to watch your face. Just watch it. What do you see there?"

Abel looked on as he sat in that past posture. There was something in him that could make a person wonder if he was even looking at what he was looking at when he was looking at it. Not that you'd think he was looking at something else, just that he might be a zero, really a zero, turned off with a switch.

He opened his mouth.

"I guess they told him to come here. He came."

"Who?"

"The man in the chair."

"That's you. Abel Cotter. Age forty-six. Sanitation worker. Born Seaport District."

"Saying who it is, you can say that. You can say that. It's a film of a person."

The woman laughed.

"Well, it happened."

"I know it happened. Something happening doesn't mean it's not fake. This is fake, for instance."

He touched the fabric of his robe.

"These aren't real clothes. Your clothes are real clothes. See, they're real. These aren't real."

"Okay. But where is he now, where is that man?"

He sighed and it seemed like it had taken all his energy to make that short outburst. Now he was returning into a familiar opacity.

"Listen, where's that man, the man you're looking at? Where is he now?"

"I don't know."

"I'm not the sort who comes at you hard. But someone who did, someone like that, they'd say to you, This is why you've had the same job for the last twenty years. Never getting anywhere. This is why you live on, on Robus Avenue. Nobody wants to live there. It's just not healthy. But that's where you live, because you close your eyes and turn away, and just bear things, just wait. And what happens? They get worse. You're always ready to opt out. Now listen. I'm not your enemy. I'm showing you how to evaluate what you see. We're not impartial. In fact, we have wagers going, every time. Could be I put a wager on you. Got it? If you listen to me you'll have better odds. You want to make it through. I want you to make it through. We both want the same thing."

"What if I don't mind being sent home?"

The girl shook her head in frustration, like she was talking to a child. "You've got to think ahead. You get sent home it isn't always the way it was. Get sent home on day one, your designation drops. Can you afford that? You want to wait longer in every line?"

"Lines are long."

"It doesn't have to be that way. If you make it to day two, or halfway through day two, could be your lot improves. Could be. Anyway, I don't like to lose. The main thing you've got is your equanimity. I can't tell if it's that or just the dumb look of a beaten animal. But if it is equanimity, you've got an actual shot, because that's what we're looking for. People never learn to be objective. Someone like you ends up there, ends up, he might end up with a piece of actual objectivity not by craft but because he thinks he's so small he can't even be taken into account."

She lapsed into silence and they sat there.

Abel watched himself being examined on the screen. The man in the chair was motionless, but still he flinched and cowered. His degradation was distributed so evenly in his body, it was practically invisible. It wasn't anything anyone would want to look at for long.

The window from the outside was low and rectangular, and the room was shallow. Probably the window was just there so you could know if someone was inside.

Abel was inside. He sat with his garment around his waist. A band had been put around his chest with some kind of transmitter on it and a metal plate with a cord running off it. A heavyset woman of about his age sat there, similarly outfitted. The plate dug into her bare breasts.

"When a symbol appears on the wall one of you will be shocked, whoever is slower."

"What?" the woman asked. "Hold on."

"We're going to ask you to tell a story, just say anything, just talk. When you get partway through, the symbol will appear, and you press the button. Okay?"

"You first, 2227900."

"Is that me? That's me. Oh."

A round button appeared on the touch screen of the tabletop. One in front of Abel, one in front of the woman.

The woman looked at him, looked at the button, looked at the wall. "Be ready. You can start your story now."

The woman opened her eyes wide and they bulged. Her eyes were a marvelous green, like bottle glass. She looked like she was drowning.

"I work in a shop that sells hologram machines. You'd be surprised who comes in to buy them. At first it was real popular and people wanted them everywhere. Okay, well, that was fine. We'd sell them. But then fewer and fewer people. And now the most popular are the ones that take the place of people, you know, you've seen them, there's no taxi driver but it seems like there's one. If it's a hypnogram, then you recognize the guy already, you know, it's great. Same thing with a room cleaner. It's on wheels, it's going around your house, but when you look at it, it looks like it's your mom, or maybe some guy you met when you were at school. Makes the world feel small."

There was a long tone, then the symbol appeared.

Abel moved his hand, then stopped. The woman slapped at the table and Abel shook.

The tone again. The symbol again. Again she shocked him. He made no move to touch the button.

"I'm sorry," she said. Her face scrunched up. She looked straight ahead at the screen.

"Continue your story," a voice said.

The woman was breathing fast. She tried to catch her breath and talk at the same time.

"A lot of people think that the hypnographs, they work the same as other holograms or projections or whatnot, but, no, it's not like that at all. They just flicker something, just parts of images, like a Rorschach blot, parts of images of a person, and they flick 'em really fast, fast as they can, and your brain just substitutes something, sticks something there from your own head. That's why it's different for . . ."

There was a long tone, then the symbol appeared.

The woman mashed at the button, but missed it, then hit at it again.

The shock ran through Abel again. He tried to take a breath and failed. He took a deep, shaky breath and shut his eyes, then opened them.

"That's it," said a voice. "It's over. We'll be in to

get you. Just sit tight." The woman was sweating and breathing heavily. She was looking at him now.

"Why didn't you press it," she said. "You fucking asshole. You asshole." She was shaking with hate.

Three officials came into the room. "Let's remove your harnesses."

Abel unhooked his, stood, put his garment back over his chest.

They were leading the woman out the other side. She was practically spitting on the floor.

"He thinks he's better than me," she said. "What a piece of shit. He thinks, he thinks . . ."

"Don't think about it," said the official. "Just stop thinking about it." Then they were gone. The other official, an older man, was waiting for him.

"There's no passing the test," the official said, turning away. "You don't gain anything by what you did."

Abel laughed, a short hoarse laugh. The official turned back to look at him.

"Excuse me?"

"Nothing."

Another official came into the room. She was very

tall, with soft shoulders like a stuffed animal, but her face was taut like a canvas.

"Is there some problem?"

The first official raised an eyebrow.

"Nothing," said Abel again.

"Tell us what's funny. What's the funny thing?"

Abel shook his head, looked at the ground.

The first official gave the second a guarded look. The second nodded. "Come along now."

"In rows of three now, line up."

On the side of a corridor they stood facing boilers stacked three high. The boilers had little doors on the front. There must have been fifty just in that hallway. The first opened at floor level. For the second and third there was a ladder.

The fans cycled off and there was a flat and immaculate silence. In the distance down the hallways someone chuckling said, "This is what you get when you win. What do you get if you lose?"

Someone else said, "I'm claustrophobic. I can't get in that."

To which someone replied, "I've used these before. When you get in, there's a program for that. It'll seem big, I tell you. You wouldn't think so, but it's true."

Another voice, "It's not a jury, it's re-education. Re-education and elimination. I'm telling you. It's political. Maybe there isn't even a criminal to begin with. Maybe nobody did anything. Maybe they think we're the ones who did it, whatever it is, the nothing they're looking for. The guy I was with in the last room got dragged off in restraints."

All at once with a creak and a hiss the boiler doors opened. There were beds inside.

"Toilets at the end of the hall. Gather in room A at seven a.m. There'll be a bell at ten to."

The two women in front of Abel were happy, adventurously happy, walking advertisements. They were like extras in a movie. One said, "Whenever I travel with my husband, we stay in these QuikStops at the train stations. I make him get his own. The poor thing thrashes in his sleep like a rhino."

"Well, my husband can never sleep if I'm not there. Tonight he'll have to make do with my projection."

The first woman laughed.

"How much time'd you give him?"

"One-hour license." She winked at the other woman. "But nothing dirty. I like to be around for the dirty parts."

Abel climbed the ladder, opened the round pod door, and went through. It was like getting into a washing machine. Inside, the bed was neat and clean. The door shut behind him and the noise of the hallway was gone. He adjusted himself, and lay looking up. After a minute he cleared his throat, then sighed, then spoke.

"Projection. Harmony, version six."

The ceiling of the little room, just inches above his head, glimmered with light and yawned open. He was looking out a window over a long meadow. The sky was there, far above. It was evening in a small town. Kids were playing in and among things like a light breeze, grass, trees, the sound of insects. A combustion car went by. Now and then the children's voices would rise in the distance.

Abel shut his eyes a minute, then opened them again. "History Companion," he said. Images bloomed up all over the ceiling. "Scroll once."

A new set appeared in their place: "Days of the Change."

Light orchestral music, slightly ominous, began and Abel was looking down on a city square. Someone was speaking to a crowd. It was a young woman, and she was whipping them into a frenzy. A voice-over came, as if from behind Abel's shoulder, and it spoke to him about the rallies and demonstrations that had led to political collapse. The camera swooped down towards the crowd and the woman's face came closer and closer. She was dressed in a slightly military fashion, and an older man, a scientist, stood behind her.

"DeTourning and her father founded Palos Chemicals the year she was thirteen. He was sixty. By nineteen she was the head researcher, answering only to him. By twenty-five, elbow-deep in politics, she gave a series of speeches that overthrew the government. This is Days of the Change."

Just as the program announced its name, it faded out. Beneath its false sky, Abel was already asleep.

JURY

[DAY 2]

There was a chair and there was a helmet on the ground next to the chair. The helmet was not connected to anything. It appeared to be made out of some hard plastic or metal but it was porcelain to the touch. He sat in the chair and he lifted it. It was heavy. It covered the whole head but for the mouth and somehow it shrank to fit. There was some plastic in it that learned. It made itself fit you. The back of the chair had divots to rest the helmet on. You lay back and sat helmeted for whatever came next.

"This is a recording of something that already happened. Do you understand? Raise your hand if you understand."

Abel raised his hand.

"When it starts you will feel a kind of rush and

you will be divorced from your body. You will be in the repeat room, but as an observer. The place that you are in was previously occupied by someone else, who made a judgment based on what they saw. This is the kind of judgment you will be led to make. Do you understand? Raise your hand if you understand."

Abel raised his hand.

"This is not the repeat room. This is not the equipment of the repeat room. It is like the repeat room and like that equipment. A simulation, based upon the reports of many previous jurors, has been put together for use in training. The repeat room itself will not be this way. Because it is a simulation, you needn't fear. You will be watching images and hearing sounds that will render for you the sort of situations that you may encounter later. The simulation is made of images and sounds, it is heard and seen. This is not the case with the repeat room, as we will explain later. Do you understand?"

Abel did not raise his hand.

"It is sufficient now for you to know that you will be involved in a very immersive environment using light and sound, and that you have nothing to fear. Do you understand?"

Abel raised his hand.

"Today is a kind of experiment, you will make a judgment. It will have no bearing, but it will be a way of feeling what it is like, and a way for us to see what it is you think and how. Do you know the criteria that you will use to judge the case? Raise your hand if you do."

Abel raised his hand.

"You will see a human scenario. You will know who is the object of your judgment. That doesn't need to be explained. You will feel it because the scenario is oriented like a dream around that person. Elements of life may be missing. Do you understand?"

Abel did not raise his hand.

"You are judging whether the person in question should be a part of our community. Whatever you think that means, that is sufficient. You may be asked later to explain your decision, but it is you who decides the basis, the sufficiency. A person can be a part of our community, or they can live within it as a hazard. This is about the removal of such hazards. Keep an eye out."

The voice kept talking, repeating variations of this. Abel would sometimes raise a hand, sometimes not. Eventually, the voice stopped and there was just a room with a helmeted man in it, blunted, noiseless. What was he listening for?

"What did you see?"

The short man from the locker room was there, seated next to him. They had been given packets of food to eat and small bottles of water. The short man had set his provisions beside him on the bench. He turned towards Abel. He had the helpless feral look of someone who wants to talk.

"Come on, we're in this together."

"Didn't we all see the same thing?"

"Well, yeah. It's obvious. They don't run it special for one person or another. There's too many total. It's got to go BAM BAM BAM like a hole punch, you know? But maybe you noticed different things than I did. There was a lot to see in there. Man, if I had one of those in my living room, I'd never go out. PTTTTTTTCHHHHFFFFF! I'd just be shooting around through the air."

Abel nodded slightly. He put the food in his mouth and chewed it. It wasn't any good trying to chew, so he swallowed.

"You know, at first I thought it might be a trick. Like, even though they said it wasn't the real thing, it was. They just want to keep you from getting scared, so they sneak you into it not knowing. So I sat down and I was just breathing and trying to say to myself, Marcus, don't let yourself vomit. Just keep it together.

"I read up ahead, get it? They say everyone who's died doing it vomited first. So I figure, don't vomit, don't die. You know?"

Abel laughed. "Well, I guess, but . . ."

"No buts, stupid, just don't vomit. That's what I read. Just listen to me. You a little slow? Am I getting through here? Anyhow, for me . . . how was it for me? The helmet starts to click and it's heavy around your head. You remember, kind of frightening. Then first thing I saw was a house like in an old movie. Like a farmhouse, but with no farm. Then I was in it. There was a lady and she was in a chair. Maybe she was seventy or eighty. I knew her, I mean, the way she was looking at me, I've woken up next to her for years. That's how it seemed."

Abel opened the water bottle, drank it down, stood, walked steadily to a garbage slot in the wall, put the dregs of his lunch through it, and returned. He sat heavily and turned to look at the man.

"So when she falls out of the chair what did you do?"

"It wasn't me doing it," said the man. "Don't you get it—it's the defendant. He's the one who does it, you're just along for the ride."

Abel uncrossed his legs and leaned a little forward.

"But it feels like I did it."

"That's how it feels, but you didn't choose anything. He chose it."

"I guess so."

"And you judge whether it was right or not. Whether it was the right thing to do."

They sat there with the noise of their breathing a little while.

"The one with the dog," said Abel.

"I never liked dogs anyway," said Marcus. "Not partial to them, you know. So which way did you go? Did you judge it right? I told them . . ."

The door opened and people called them through it.

"Five-seven-three-two-eight, come to station twelve."

He sat in a large room. He was by himself on one

side. Other people had been coming in and after a while people continued on. On the other side there was a counter of gleaming white steel. Some guards were behind it. There was an old sign on the wall that said INTAKE.

One of the guards was calling to him and gesturing. It seemed like it had been going on for a while.

"Five-seven-three-two-eight to INTAKE station twelve. Move along."

Abel stood at the counter. Two men faced him. They stood so he could look at only one of them at a time.

"Your dossier mentions a child."

Abel shook his head slightly.

"You had a child, you and your wife, did you not? Speak in the negative or affirmative."

"I had a child, yes."

"Where is that child, what was it?"

"It was a boy. What happened, well . . ." His voice trailed off.

"We want you to say it," said the other man. "We want to hear you say what happened."

Abel tried to say, but it caught in his throat. He just stood there. The man shook his fist in Abel's face.

"You don't know what good this is, what good that is, you just do what we say. Now tell us, what happened to your boy."

Abel dragged it out and said it.

"There was a knock at the door. Government people were there. Someone had called them on us, one of the neighbors."

"And . . ."

"My wife and I, we were deemed incompetent, emotionally incompetent, culturally incompetent."

"Ha, culturally incompetent. That's a laugh. That's a low bar to fail at. Don't even know enough to watch a television."

"They made you D3A?"

Abel nodded. He ran his hand over his forehead, as if wiping something, but there wasn't anything to wipe.

"And you're still D3A?"

Abel didn't say anything. The other man laughed.

"Of course he is, they don't unD3A you." He reached across the counter and clapped Abel on the shoulder. "So they took your boy, they took your baby, your little kid, they took him, huh? How old was he?"

"A month old," said the other one. "Says here, one month."

"And then your wife left you. Course she did. And you work on a garbage truck. Nice. Nice life. One day you think you're going to astronaut school, next you know you're, well, you're you. How's that? You think you were going to astronaut school, buddy? You think that?"

"It's beside the point anyway," said the second man. "Point is, your child, if he lived, how old would he be. Do you know? It's easy math."

"Eighteen, nineteen," said Abel. "I don't think about it."

One of the men went to the other and whispered something in his ear. They both laughed.

"Well, over on this side of the counter we've got to wonder, this case, it's a kid, you see. He's about your son's age. We wouldn't want you making any mistakes. Conflict of interest. You get what I mean? We're guys like you. We've got your interest at heart. Heck, Jack here's D3A too, isn't that right, Jack?"

Jack shook his head.

"You piece of shit, you're the one who's D3A."

"I'm just trying to help the guy. And pass the time. Let's look at this another way. How about . . ."

"Aww, let the poor bastard go. He's going to fail out. Look at him."

A tone sounded in the background. A door opened. Marna came in. She saw Abel's expression.

"You lot giving it to him? Don't listen to them," she said.

The two men laughed. One patted her on the arm. "You know we wouldn't do that."

"Right, right. The door's this way."

Abel stood a moment longer. He leaned into the counter. "Was this official? Cause it seems like maybe, like . . ."

The men laughed.

"We're just supposed to tell you to head on. That's all. When the time's up, we say, 'Head on.' But some of us like to look at the dossiers, like to check things out, see what's going on. Helps to pass the time."

The men laughed. The other one broke in.

"Thing is, what's official, what's not, who's to say?"

"It all goes in your record. You know that if you know anything."

"Pretty soon you'll have a record the length of my arm."

One of the men held out his arm for Abel to look at, but it was just an arm like anyone's.

Now Abel was back in the examination room again. He was back in the sloping chair. The same three officials looked at him over the same table.

"Round two," said the man with the beard.

"We have some questions for you," said Ella.

A nurse came into the room with a small medical unit on wheels. He attached some of the cords to Abel.

"It monitors the temperature of your skin," continued Ella. "The injection makes you a bit more eager to talk. That's it. It just loosens the tongue. Someone like you could probably use a steady drip."

The nurse asked Abel for his arm. The arm was given, and once it was given it was held in two hands, put in an appropriate position, wrapped, tightened, injected. This happened and meanwhile Abel sat there staring straight forward.

"All done," said the nurse.

"We have a set group of questions. These are questions we ask everyone at this stage, so do not take offense."

"First question," said the bearded man, "describe your home."

Abel closed his eyes and opened them. He looked at the table between Ella and the third official. His gaze settled there and stayed.

"Two ways you can enter it. One is the bathroom window, which leads to a fire escape. Other is the front door, which leads out onto a landing. Many doors there. It's the third from the stairs. The other people are fairly loud. They carry on in the stairwell, so my side of the door has thick cardboard on it. I put it there. I remember the day I took the place, I tried to rent it from the woman without seeing it, but she wanted me to see it. We went upstairs together and she went in first and she showed it to me. I said, I'll take it. She said, you haven't even looked around. I said, it is just like the others. She said, they're all good apartments, but this is the one will be yours. Since then it's been mine, that's about fifteen years. No one else in the building has been there so long."

"That's good," said Ella. "What is it like in your house?"

"There's a bed that folds into the wall. There's a table like that too. Mostly they both stay out, since there's no call to put them up. There's a shower in the corner, and a toilet in the other corner, with a curtain. The curtain stays where it is. I don't believe I have ever closed it."

"Have you ever brought people to your house? What is that like?"

"Once," said Abel.

"And what was it like?"

"I would prefer I guess to keep that to myself."

One of the examiners said, "Was it a woman?" at the same time as another said, "Was it a man?"

"My wife came once."

"Ex-wife."

"Yes, my ex-wife, she came once. She wanted to borrow some money. Things weren't good for her."

"And she's dead now, isn't she?"

Abel closed his eyes. He opened them. He looked at the ceiling. It was seamless. Just a thin coat of nothing on a meaningless surface. At that moment it contained him.

"She's dead, all right."

"The records say she took her life. Do you know why?"

Abel didn't answer. He touched the sensor on his arm with the other arm.

"Don't touch that. Kristof."

The technician stepped up, took his arm again, adjusted the sensor. He nodded and stepped away.

"Please stay still."

"Your wife is dead. She's dead. Do you know why?"

Ella spoke up. "Just tell us how you found out. What was that day like?"

"I was coming back from work. The food delivery was outside, and so I stopped to take my allotment, a one-month crate, and the guy looked at me funny. He said, You're Cotter, right? I said yes, he said you have an ex by the name of Elaine lives by the Garden stop? I said yes, how do you know? He said, I used to talk to her when she lived here, then she lived there. Now she's dead. I saw them taking the body out of the house. I told him thanks, and took the crate and went inside. I sat on the bed and tried to remember her, but all I could remember was what my friend said the day I met her."

"What friend? What did he say?"

"He said, isn't that the girl Cen used to go with? I remembered it ever since."

The three examiners left the room. The lab tech disconnected the cords and rolled his device out the door.

The carpet was a yellowish color, similar to the robe. Abel looked at his bare foot against the ground, and then looked at the wall where the mirror was.

A humming sound came then, and the wall lit up with a projection. It was the image of the man in the cell. He was asleep.

The quality of this projection was grainy because the light in the cell was low. The man had turned his face to the wall and his arm was curled partially around his body like a victim in a painting.

Abel got off the chair and sat on the floor and looked up at the man. At that moment the man woke, and he turned and looked back at the camera. He began to cry and he hid his face. There was no sound in this projection. In the empty room, there was just the sound of someone breathing, and that person was Abel. The projection was hardly real. It was a projection specifically because it was not a real person. It could not be both.

The man in the cell lay down and turned his back and it was immediately apparent that he had not been sleeping at all in the beginning, but had been lying there in much the same condition, unable to sleep, unable to stand, unable to lie, unable to sit. Anything probably felt like a hopeless compromise.

Abel got up and went to the door. It was open. He went out into the hall and Marna was there waiting.

"Come with me," she said.

Abel was back in room A. It was largely empty now. Just a few people here and there, some of them lying on their backs on the benches. He put his arms on his knees and rested his head in his hands, shut his eyes. The student Joan was there on the far side. After a while, she came over.

"Hey," she said.

He opened his eyes.

"Rough time, huh?" She touched her nose as if to check if it was still there. "That helmet made me woozy."

He nodded.

"No, really. I hate all that shit, projections, holograms, whatnot. That's why I want to see the repeat room. It isn't like that at all."

"No?"

She leaned in.

"They say it's not even technological. I've heard someone found it."

Abel shook his head. "I'd bet it's like the rest of this stuff. It's the way the world is."

"Yeah, maybe. I did some drawings of the session while I was waiting here. They brought me some paper when I asked. Want to see?"

She handed him some sheets of paper. He unfolded them carefully.

"Yeah," he said. "This was the worst of it."

He was holding a drawing of a body floating in a pool.

"Do you think they show you a bad case first to prepare you?" he asked.

She nodded.

"I guess so. I guess. But, I don't know, do you get the sense that maybe they don't even know what they're doing, whether they're doing it right or not?"

Abel laughed.

"Place like this they can't possibly know what's actually going on. Matter of fact, they only check to see when something's wrong."

He held up a drawing. This one was of a colony of ants teeming out of a crack in the sidewalk.

"I don't remember this," he said.

"I didn't see that. It's just how I felt when we watched the woman drown. You see, when I was a kid I used to pour hot water on anthills. I don't know why. I'm pretty embarrassed of it now, but it was what I did. Way back then."

"Kids don't know what they're doing," said Abel. "They're like hands without faces."

"I don't know. I feel like it's the same as it ever was. I'm still that way. I'm the last to know what's happening to me, who's doing it, or why. And if I do it, if I do something, I find out I'm doing it as it happens. Isn't it that way for you?"

Abel's hands were playing with the cloth of his gown, worrying at it.

"See," she said. "Look, you ripped it. Bet you didn't mean to."

A man led Abel to a concrete stairway. He was average height, about Abel's age. He had his I.D. card in his hands. He was playing with it compulsively.

"This way," the man said, pointing upwards. "It leads to the roof."

On the wall of the stairwell were written many

aphorisms about justice in clean black paint on a white background. There were longer ones and shorter, one for each step.

Some said, We must endeavor to be sure of what we do not know.

Man's house is built from the bodies of his neighbors, and all who are living lift it together.

Most dogs howl when they see something like the moon, but a blind dog howls only at the moon.

The text of the final one just about ringed the molding of the door:

A fair judge knows a goatherd from a swineherd. A good judge knows the smell of a shepherd from the smell of a butcher. A great judge knows the smell of a doctor from the smell of a priest. But it is a poor judge who believes the speech of her nose.

"You know why they put these here?" the man asked.

Abel shook his head.

"It's not to give you the principles, it's just to, just, how do I put it? It's to give you the feeling there's a tradition. You're part of a tradition if you're a juror. We take that seriously. These used to be on the walls

all over the complex, but people got tired of staring at them. I guess they missed these when they
repainted."

They emerged onto a kind of parapet. From it the
unnerving city wheeled in broad circles.

"Name's Marcus, Marcus Gopp. I bring you all up
here to tell about the time I was a juror."

He held up his identification card. It said 59j. Abel
reached for it unconsciously.

"It's okay. Here, have a look."

Marcus let Abel hold the I.D. card for a minute.

"Never seen one like that before, eh? Yeah, I remember when I was like that. It's been a while,
though. So listen. I do the introductions one by one.
It's valuable, my time is valuable, but if you turn out
to be a juror too, your time is valuable also. You get
it? It's an investment. Do you want to hear?"

"I do."

"It was about ten years ago, right at the start. I
mean, I must have been one of the very first. There
was a feeling back then, perhaps you remember it. It
was like—maybe the whole thing would be thrown
out. Maybe it didn't work at all. It's hard to remember

people used to feel that way, but there it was. Part of the NEW SOCIETY INITIATIVE. Everything changed at the same time."

He laughed uneasily.

"There was a lot of violence. I mean, it was a political changeover, a new epoch, right? Any case, we all had heard about it, THE REPEAT ROOM. You get the gray envelope brought to your door, and that's it. I couldn't believe it happened to me already. Nobody I know had ever gone, not like today, when half the people have been brought in and failed out. So I didn't know what to expect, not exactly. Anyway, I was brought in, not to this building, but to the one that stood here before. It was smaller. They hadn't brought the people over from the previous system, instead they started from scratch, like I was saying, so it was small at first. I came in early morning time, like you're supposed to, stood in line. There was a big auditorium. The clerks would call us one by one and we would go up and sit on the stage, in front of everyone. They were proving how safe the thing was too, you know. Health concerns. So you'd sit there with the helmet on in front of everyone, and then afterwards they would ask you what you thought. The audience couldn't hear you, but they could see you were all right. When my number was called, my knees just shook. Don't think I ever did anything in front of fifty people before, let alone a hundred like it was then. Now it's a thousand. Things march on, I guess. Well, I got to the stage and I sat down and I couldn't get the helmet to fit right. I've always had a big head, and I thought that was it, but it turns out there was a short. There was no juice to it. So once they fixed that, the thing slipped on perfectly. I forgot all about the auditorium, let me tell you. And that was just the practice. Later on, when they'd winnowed us down, there were just three of us left. That's how they did it then, three people, and whichever way two of 'em go, well, that's it. At that point, there's three helmets they bring out and you sit next to each other. I remember one of the other two was young, maybe twenty-two, and I thought to myself, this guy can't know how to choose any better than me. It gave me some confidence, you know. At that time, they had you meet the accused. You actually met them before you judged them. They were working on different ways to make it feel severe. I mean, to make it so you don't take it lightly. Anyway, you're probably wondering why I took you out of the line, brought you up here. Everybody's getting to talk to someone at one point or another. They learned that it helps the process. What's the word? Humanizes it. Reason they picked me to talk to you now is because the scenes you saw earlier were imagined from the judgment I did. It was a woman, about forty. I know now that she had killed her neighbor, but they don't tell you at the time, since it shouldn't matter what they did. But as you saw, she didn't have an ounce of human in her. Every scene she does the worst thing. Bit after bit, you feel your heart slide. Well, they killed her, ten years ago now, and it was my fault, or my honor as they say. I've thought about it plenty, and I think it is the right system, the right way to go about it. My misgivings have grown smaller, year by year, and now I can't find them no matter where I look. You know which one did it for me? Do you? It wasn't the pool. Somehow the real bad things, I understand how a person could freeze up. No, it was the crossing guard jag. You look down at your chest and you see, oh, I guess that's it, I stand here at the street and the kids cross. I mean, this happens nowhere, but it used to, I guess? Roads and automobiles with, what do they call them, hood ornaments? Well, you see you're a crossing guard, and the kids are coming from a blind street, the cars can't see 'em. The kids are having some kind of race, dumb like kids are, just flinging themselves into the space in front of them, no idea what's to come of it, and it's time to tell the cars to stop, and you feel, you know, the woman I was judging, you feel her hesitate, just a little, hesitate to stop the cars. That was it for me. Right then, I knew: she's got to be let go. We can't have a person like that walking the streets. Now, that's not to say I don't sometimes do the wrong thing, we all do. But you've got to look out for each other. Without that, what's left? So that's how it was for me. It, well, it just wasn't that bad at all."

"But . . ." Abel kicked at the roof with his foot. "But what was it like?"

"It's not images, it's not a film. It's more like knowing something. Knowing something, it isn't a picture. It isn't a sound, right?"

The pathway on the rooftop was pretty dirty and the roof was too. The streets below were dirty. Filth blew back and forth in the city, covering everything that wasn't already covered up. Just standing there, they were in it.

"I guess it doesn't seem efficient. All this seems like a lot for one criminal."

"Well, they see it as education, and as a kind of, they call it, winnowing. In the process of the jury, they discover other people who are unfit. That's how you can come in to be on a jury and end up being prosecuted yourself. So it's like they're going through the population and weeding them out, a thousand at a time. They end up with a few hundred at the new social baseline; those get a new designation. The others are downgraded. That's the real progress. The society is shifting in plain sight from one kind of group to another, and people don't even realize it's happening."

Marcus shaded his eyes.

"It'd be nice to have a different designation, wouldn't it? The way they feel, if they go through the whole population once this way, everything will improve. Then there's a second pass, and a third pass. Right now it's only a capital crime can bring you in here. I've seen the charts, they say in one hundred years, might be just stealing gets you removed. They say removed because it's a boat, you know. We're on the boat together, you get it?"

Abel sat on his heels out of the wind. He looked up at Marcus.

"I'm sorry. I still don't get the difference. The actual thing, the helmet. When it's on, the real one, if it isn't like the simulation, well, then, what is it like?"

Marcus put his hands in his pockets and leaned back on his legs.

"The simulation is just for you to imagine. But the real thing is the real thing. It's not in terms of something else. It is something else. You follow? You're in their head. You're not in your head, you're in their head."

"I don't . . ."

"You're worrying about it. Don't worry about it. If you end up there, you'll see. We can talk about it afterwards, over a cold one."

"So now you just get up in the morning, come here, and talk to people?"

"For ten years. They give you your choice of work. But this is what I like. I got it one day, just woke up thinking: I like the people I look at, and if I don't like them, I learn why, and then I do. It's a specialty I have."

Abel spat on the ground.

"Well, you know, there's a mountain of garbage we move out of here every day."

"I don't doubt it. Keeps the city running, and that's not a shame. If you pass this thing, they'll move you on to something else. They'll think you're too valuable for that."

Marcus patted Abel on the shoulder.

"I'm going to take you over to the judgment room, just so you can see it."

In the waiting area outside the judgment room, there was a film to watch. It began with a lot of grass, well mowed. Someone was riding a horse on it, a woman in tailored clothes. She got down off the horse and approached the camera. Up close you could see she was typical-perfect, face built up like a leopard, but she was old enough to have lines at the corners of her eyes. That made you trust her. She smiled an exciting smile straight at you and said to the camera,

"The way forward is not through punishment. In the world we are choosing, there won't be any punishment. Telleman called it the punitive principle, it's what we've moved past. Instead, we simply predict who can act well, who will act well. Those who cannot, we remove. It is a constant process."

A man walked on-screen. He was carrying a wooden binocular case over his shoulder. He was distinguished-looking, with a short, well-trimmed beard of silver gray. His eyebrows were black and dense. He wore a boating jacket and cloth trousers.

"Fewer and fewer people will have to work. Mechanization and algorithmic control mean freedom to just participate in the act of being human. More and more we see that what that means is deciding who gets to be human."

The woman cut in.

"We're social creatures. Thousands of years ago, we foraged and scavenged in packs and in tribes. We had to go on foot together over impossibly brutal landscapes. But even then the main thing wasn't just how you could accomplish your needs. It was always, how do you situate yourself with others, how do you as a person fit in the social order?"

The man sighed in a happy way. The woman looked at him adoringly. "That's the real genius of it. After hundreds of thousands of years, we found a way to pick out who deserves to live. And, we realized, that act of picking is itself the real role you get to play as a person. Your whole life up until now has been an audition for this moment."

The two people twined around and walked away across the yard. The screen went dark and the lights came on, revealing the same room they had been in. It was the room in which the film had been about to happen, and after the film, it was the room in which the film had happened. You were put back in your body again.

Marcus was next to him. He said, "Let's go and look at the judgment room."

The door was unlocked and they went through. The judgment room was about the size of a community theater. They entered at the back of where the audience would be, but there were no chairs for an audience. There was just a bench at one end, and then an empty space, and then a stage. On the stage there was a concrete box. On one side was a door with a wheel mechanism to shut it, a wheel mechanism like on a boat. The door hung open, and it was at least a foot thick, solid metal. Just looking at it could make a person ill.

"They've talked about eventually broadcasting

this process. People'll sit in their houses and watch the whole thing. But that's not where we're at yet. I think it'd be frightening. People would be frightened even to come down here. So we bring them in, just a few at a time. Get it? As for the accused, well, they bring the accused in there. You see the circle? That's where the criminal stands. Now you, you're sitting there, on the bench. At this point in time, it's just you. Before it was you and the other two, that's how I saw it. When they bring the accused in, it's through that door. The guards have a kind of pole with a loop on it. The end's around the neck of the defendant, so they don't have to be close. You know, a safe distance. Each of them has a pole, and they stand on either side with the poles almost crossing. That way there's nothing the defendant can do but listen. Here, listen to this."

The man shouted, a short loud meaningless shout.

"You can hear my voice carry in here. Can you hear it? Well, it's quiet, and you're standing there trying not to mess up, and someone from the back, says, 'We record the verdict in case number . . . ,' and then they say the case number. Then it's on you. You say, I mean they tell you how, and you practice, you say, 'In case 33912 of the new epoch, I, juror Gopp of the jury Gopp, Lewin, Jackson, declare the accused,' well, in my case her name was Laura Salvatore, 'declare the accused Laura Salvatore to be unfit for the community.' She doesn't get to say anything. Anyway, her mouth is covered, so she couldn't even if she wanted to. They push her into the room with the poles and when she's in there, they keep pushing and just let go of the poles, leave them inside. They close the door and turn the wheel. They're turning it and turning it, it seems like forever. Finally they're done. That's when the clock starts. How long can you hold your breath? Some people can hold it a long time. So you wait a long time. You wait on that bench for an hour. Then they wheel open the door and grab the poles again. They walk backwards holding the poles and the accused, who became the condemned, and is now just, well, isn't anything anymore, is dragged back out. I don't know, in my case, she was just the way she went in, but dead. Sometimes, they say, they bang their head out on the wall and you have to clean it up. I mean, you don't have to. Someone does."

Abel sat in room A for an hour and for another hour and for another. The candidates were taken out in ones and twos. Some came back, some didn't. It seemed like there was a way to fail even the briefing. Whether there was a way or not, people were finding it.

The woman next to him, with a huge aquiline nose and small eyes, was telling a story to a man with a monstrous belly. He held the belly like he was pregnant and watched the woman talk.

She said, "That's the game."

"But I don't see how that is a game. I mean, what is there to do?"

"You just do whatever you want to do, but everything's real different because, you see, everyone knows who you are without you even meeting them, get it?"

The man did not get it. He told her he didn't get it.

"From the beginning, you get there to this little town. It's a retreat town, that's what they call it, or a vacation town, something like that. It costs a lot of money. People do this as a big gift, for retirement, or graduation, something like that. I got it for retirement, retired early, a few years early. It was part of the package. One day I'm at my desk as usual, a week later, my husband and I are pulling into this vacation town. Now, before you go there, their people visit you and take a bunch of notes, speak to you, photograph you, find out all your preferences. Then when you arrive, everyone in the town knows you. You get to pick how that is, but I picked that I was on a popular show, a game show. I was the host. So they work with you on that, work out what that was like. Then when you get out of your car, people are taking pictures of you, people are asking for your autograph. You sit down at a restaurant and it's, 'How do you deal with the fame?' from the bartender, and you're saying, 'I just pretend I'm a regular person and maybe I am,' or some other crock of shit. It's a good time."

"I just feel," said the man, resting his elbow on his belly and scratching his chin, "I feel it's not for me."

"I thought that too," said the woman, "but there's something hypnotic about having everyone pretend not to watch you. It's a wonderful feeling."

After a while, some attendants brought them water. Somebody asked for food and was told they were fasting.

"Fasting why?"

"I don't give the answers," the guy said.

"Well, who does?"

"Just sit there and wait like you're told."

Soon it had been another hour and another. The light was gone from the high windows on the edges of the room. They were just in it now, in this tank of a room, waiting for what?

After a while, the lights came on.

The medical intake had been there all along, at the other end of room A, but they had never been told to go that way, and so none of them had. Now they were in a line, about fifty of them, stood up like dominos, pointing towards the double glass doors.

On the screen above their heads, a projection was playing.

A woman in surgical clothing and a hairnet came casually onto the screen. "Good news, you've made it this far. That means you're all decent people. Truly."

She winked.

"You'll all be designated JJ. That means real potential jurors. It's the best news you've heard yet. I'll give you a moment to congratulate yourselves."

Some shouted. Some hugged the one next to them. Others looked at the wall. It was a great relief, it seemed, to those who stood in the line. Abel could see Joan up ahead, near the front. All the others he had spoken to were gone. The man behind him touched the small of his back in a friendly way.

"Can you believe it?"

Abel made a noise that didn't mean anything.

But people really were overjoyed. They were sputtering and gibbering like turkeys with human mouths.

"It's like when they used to have that, what did they call it? The number game? What was that?"

This was a real heavyset gentleman speaking up, not really knowing what to say, but speaking up all the same.

"The lottery," someone else said.

"Yeah, it's like the lottery. It's like we won the lottery. My wife will be so—"

The same fellow interrupted. "Maybe you can't go back to her. She's a lower designation now. You'll have to find somebody new."

"Can't go back to her? To my wife? Shit, I never thought of that."

"There's a lot to think of."

The screen flashed to call attention to itself, and the woman continued.

"You'd like to know what happens now, wouldn't you? Well, I'm Doctor Eberhart. I work in the medical lab. I might not be there today, but I'm there most days, and so if you don't see me, you can know, it's the kind of place I like to be, and I welcome you. My job, and the job of the others there, is to do some tests on you. It's the final thing. We've weeded out all the reprobates from the juror population and now we have to see who is physically fit enough for the injections necessary to use the repeat room. We want to make sure every care is taken of you, and here's why: because you are the real citizens of our country, vetted and clean. You get it? You're the whole reason this thing goes on. Well, one by one you can start to walk forward into the Medical Intake. See you in a few!"

Inside the glass doors, there were many cubicles, perhaps forty or fifty. At each cubicle sat a person dressed in the manner of Dr. Eberhart. As the jurors came in, they sat at any available cubicle. Abel walked past seven or eight that were occupied, and a young man called to him from across the row. He went there.

The young man had eyes that were so pale you had to look for them. You had to look for his eyes in the place where eyes are.

"You've got my congratulations, that's for sure. I'm jealous, actually. There's no guarantee that I'll even make it this far, when I get selected. I'm just a medical tech, after all. Truth be told, I hope I don't. You see a lot of things, if you know what I mean. But it's not like I can avoid it. They choose you, they choose you, and that's it."

The man put out his hand to shake Abel's. They shook, and it was a firm handshake.

"Well," said the man, "you've got a heck of a hand on you there. Manual laborer, eh? I've always felt a little humiliated, to be honest, when I shake a hand like that. Like less of a man, you know. I bet you could just squeeze all the juice out of an orange with one hand. Can you?"

Abel smiled in embarrassment and shook his head.

"I'll ask you to lie down here so we can move right along. After all, we're on a schedule. You can remove the gown. No modesty here."

Abel hesitated.

"Remove your gown."

The man took Abel's vitals and connected various cords to parts of Abel's body. There was something in his throat, something around his head, an intravenous cord, a temperature monitor for his rectum, and others.

"I'll tell you what I'm going to do, and then I'm going to do it. Nothing is going to be done to you without me saying first what it is. Got it?"

"Yes."

"I'm hooking a bag up to the intravenous cord that

runs into the vein in your arm. The contents of this bag will be added to your bloodstream, or the part of it that is heading back towards your heart. When it gets there, it will go out again through your arteries and be distributed throughout your body. What is it? We call it the cocktail. It's not one thing, it's about nine things."

The man lifted up the container that the bag had come in. There was very small text all over one side of it.

"That's the information there, and you're free to read it if you want. Most people don't. I can give you the short version if you want it. Do you?"

"Yeah."

"Your body just isn't prepared for the task. The helmet they put on you actually doesn't do anything at all. It's just to protect your brain. So you put the helmet on and they stick you right by the repeat room. You're outside it, actually, but right next to it. Then the prisoner goes in, and it happens, and well, this cocktail helps your body to bear the strain."

Abel didn't seem to like that. The tech saw it.

"Oh, no no no no no no no. It's nothing to be

worried about now. Really. In the past, the system just wasn't worked out. That's when it was a problem. Now, well, now it's a question of if you can bear the cocktail. The hope is, we get thirty or forty people in here, and maybe one or two of them can handle it. The one who can is the juror, if there's two, well, we use one for the next case. If there's none, we do it all again."

Abel lay there naked on the gurney. His mouth moved, trying to formulate his uncertainty.

"But what happened before? Why'd they start doing it this way?"

"It was just too much, you know. I mean, too much for a person. The body has basic limits. I don't really know the details. Ready?"

"Hold on, what does it mean if you can't bear the cocktail?"

"Just a reaction, just a simple reaction. And let's say it does get bad, let's say worst-case scenario you end up at death's door. Not that it happens often. But occasionally, you know, things really go south, your body sees itself as the enemy, autoimmune frenzy, well, in a case like that, you're in the best possible place, right here in expert medical hands. Don't worry."

The man leaned over and peered down into Abel's face. "Here goes!"

Abel woke up in a daze and sat up on the gurney. He put his arm down for balance. The tech was smiling and looking at him. His happiness was extreme.

"You see," he said, "if we get the one who's the positive, we get a bonus."

Abel looked out of the cubicle.

"The one that's the positive?"

He could see into several other areas. People were lying on their backs on gurneys. None of them were moving. The atmosphere was quiet. The tech touched a microphone on his lapel and spoke into it. Footsteps rang out, coming towards them.

"Yeah, the positive. The one who makes it. We're going to monitor you for a few more minutes. Just be patient. You've done a great job. Your work for today is all done. Tomorrow is a big day. The biggest, but for today, well, just take it easy. If you feel anything wrong, just say so. Do you feel okay?"

"I feel fine."

"Here, let me disconnect a few of these. We're going to get you some new clothes, some different clothes. No more robes like that for you, you're done. And tonight you'll sleep in a regular room. Only the best for you now. Here they are. Hello, Doctor."

Abel woke up in a daze and sat up on the gurney. It was all he could do to stay upright. The tech was smiling happily.

"Ha ha!" he said. "There you are."

"You're in a good mood."

"Oh, I am, I am," said the tech. "You see, I'm about to get a bonus."

"A bonus?"

"Just relax. Don't worry about anything. Look at you, you beauty. Just lie down."

Abel sat on the gurney. Two women faced him. One was Dr. Eberhart. The other was Marna. They didn't say anything, they just looked at him. Eberhart asked a series of sharp questions to the tech, who answered them, one after the other. With each answer, she nodded. She stepped forward and performed an examination of Abel. If anything, she was more thorough than the tech had been. Through this, Marna watched.

"What about the rest of them?" Abel asked. The doctor ignored him.

"Please don't talk," said the tech.

"Why?"

"Just lie down again. Just lie quietly; it's not worth talking at this point."

"I want to know about the others."

The ones he could see weren't moving.

"Listen," said the doctor, "even in the best cases, you're not going to remember what we say to you right now. So it's not worth talking. Just wait it out. You'll get your answers."

The examination continued. The doctor spoke out notes to the tech, who recorded them. Occasionally Abel interrupted, and asked the same questions.

Finally they unhooked him from the machines. Marna went away.

After an hour, she came back. She had clothing which she set on a small table. Abel opened his eyes. He looked around. The scene was the same as before. "What about the rest of them?"

"They'll wake up in a while," said the doctor.

"They always wake up by tomorrow," said Marna. "No one's ever actually injured. I mean, rarely."

"We stay by them the whole night," said the tech. "Each person is monitored carefully. You don't need to worry."

The doctor walked a little ways away with Marna, said something to her. They both returned.

"It's time," said the doctor. "Put these garments on, get comfortable, and when you're ready, you'll come with us."

Abel sat in a well-appointed room. There were flowers on the table. Marna was there, along with the others from his examination.

Abel wore plain gray trousers and a gray shirt. Over the shirt he had a light coat, a sort of lab coat, with pockets in it. That was gray too.

"I'm Ludwig," said one of the men from the examination. He was the fleshier one.

He put something on the table and slid it to Abel. "This is your new I.D."

Abel looked at it, but made no move to pick it up.

"Look at it."

He was looking at it. What he saw was his name and a new designation: 2314j.

"You know what this means, don't you?"

The other man had come around the table. He put his arm around Abel. "No more garbage-picking for you. Seems like the old cultural selection really miscarried, giving you the kind of life you've had. And it's a hell of a shame about your kid. In any case, going forward, you're going to have your choice of living situations, your choice of jobs. You see, we know the kind of person you are now. Most of the population are still question marks."

"He still has to make it through tomorrow, Willis."

"That's right," said Willis. "You still have to make it through tomorrow. Which is something we all did. It's something Marna did. It's something I did. It's something Ludwig did."

Ludwig laughed.

"I let my man off. So did you, Willis. But Marna put her guy in the ground, didn't you, Marna? Buried him without remorse."

Willis laughed too. He still had his arm around

Abel in an uncomfortable way. "Marna believes in the selection part of selection."

She rolled her eyes.

"They're joking, but they're not joking. However that may be, you'll make your own choice tomorrow, and it will be based on a situation of such gravity, I can't explain it. You'll feel it. I know the film they showed you was a bit silly. The design team used to be pretty archaic. But the main points are really true. We are choosing a new society. That's the thing. We're going through the population one by one and thousand by thousand and finding the seeds for an actual civilization. Up until now there's just been barbarism. Even the last centuries, barbarism, masked by modernity."

"Do I decide in the repeat room?"

Willis inclined his head.

"You don't go in the repeat room. You've been told that, don't you remember? You are just outside of it, just off to one side. Believe me, you don't want to be any closer."

Marna continued.

"The decision is given after the repeat room. You

go to a room nearby, just a couple chairs and a table, much like this one actually"—she made a gesture with her hand—"and you sit and think. There's a couch there too. Is there? Is there a couch there?"

Ludwig nodded.

"There's a couch there," she said, "if you need to lie down. After a while, maybe an hour, we send over someone to talk to you if you're the talking kind, if you want a person to bounce ideas off. There are rules about that, a kind of framework. We'll explain it, but the person can't help you decide. They're just there to hear you talk. Sometimes it helps. You sit there anyway, and you come up with your decision, and an explanation of it. The helper records that. Once that's done, you go out to the judgment room. You've seen it, you were there earlier. You read the judgment you made."

Willis pulled out the chair next to Abel and sat in it.

"Actually, before you read the judgment, they bring in the accused. You'll see him come in. Heck, you've been looking at film of him all along. He'll be under guard. You need have no concern about that. Then once he's there, they position him just right and you read the judgment. We say 'read the judgment to the accused,' but it isn't really to the accused, it's just reading the judgment."

"Why is that?"

"Well, if it's a judgment of death, then the accused will soon be blotted out. At that point it was really that you read the judgment to the other people who were standing there, if you know what I mean. You read the judgment of life to the accused. The judgment of death just gets read aloud."

Abel didn't appear to understand completely.

"But what is it like?" asked Abel. "What is it like in the repeat room for the accused? What do they say when they come out?"

They continued telling Abel things, but it was clear to everyone that it was not worthwhile to continue. The man was practically falling out of his chair. After all, he had been injected with all manner of things and dragged from here to there and there to here. It was time to take him to his bed, and so they did that. Someone pushed a button. After a little while, an attendant came, and they led Abel away. They led him up hallways and down hallways to a room with a window. It was a sort of suite with a bath in it, sofas, a kitchen area. And no one would ask him to leave. All they did was show him where the controls were. Then they went away, and Abel lay on the bed in all his clothes and shut his eyes.

After a few hours, the man on the bed, Abel, woke. The lights were on. He sat up and looked around. Sitting on a chair was a woman. It was Marna. She was watching a hologram that was sitting in a chair also. It was the man from the prison cell.

"Someone is with you at all times until you're through here," she said. "You're too valuable to be left alone."

"Too valuable," he said, shaking his head.

"And here is your object," she said, pointing to the man. "It seems he can't sleep either."

"Can you turn him off?"

"I don't think it's possible. It's part of the general program."

Abel went into the bathroom and washed his face. He stared into the mirror. He came out of the bathroom and sat on the bed facing her. The hologram was gone from the other chair.

"Does the juror sleep easily most times?"

"I haven't been the one to sit here before," said

Marna, "so I don't know, but I think there's something in the fluids you were given, something that makes you sleep. At least, the rest of them are still sleeping, that's for sure."

"When do they wake up?"

"Anywhere from three to five days. It's funny, people come out a little thinner than they went in. But it's not unusual for the juror to wake up in the night."

"Why do you think that?"

"They told me what to do if you did. So they thought it was a possibility."

"And what was that?"

"I'm supposed to show you a film of the thing itself. We film it every time. There's an archive. I'm to show you one, just so you see what it's like. To be prepared."

Abel extended his arm in a kind of well-then-let's-have-it motion.

"By all means."

Marna sat up in her chair and said in a stiff voice, "Projection, Prepared Film."

A screen lowered about six feet past the bottom of the bed.

The lights snapped out and a projection glowed

there on the white fabric. It was a room, one he had not been in. The camera was pointed at the ground and then at the ceiling and then it turned slowly to take in the whole of the place. The walls were metal of some sort. There was equipment with various stations and readout screens. On the far side of the room was a metal box like a nautilus or like a kind of hut or shack, one that had been ravaged by time into organic shape. Beside the hut was a chair like the chair he had sat in. It was at the very side of the hut, practically touching it. A helmet was on the chair. In the side of the hut there was a small door. That side of the room was empty of things. It had the look of a derelict factory. It seemed people didn't cross it unless they had to. Now people were coming in. A naked woman was being pushed on by two guards using the same pole system Abel had seen before. She passed by close to the camera and looked at it. Her young face was bent with fear. Her neck was red where the nooses of the poles rubbed. They led her on but their pace slowed as they crossed the room and at some point it became clear the woman was resisting as much as she could. Finally she fell to her knees and lay on the ground. She refused to go on. The guards came up beside her, one on each side, and lifted her bodily. Bodily they dragged her to the door. They opened the door. When the door opened, she came alive and tried to pull herself free, she raved and tore at herself and at the guards, but it was useless. In she went and the door shut. The guards hurried back across the room as fast as they could and stood, panting, in the violence of what had happened. The film had seemed silent, but it had just been dead quiet and now the panting of the guards was in the room where Abel and Marna watched. Next came the juror, in from the back of the room, a woman with heavy braids that hung down her back. She crossed the room slowly as the others had done. When she reached the halfway point, she halted and looked back. Her voice was tiny in the space, a thin prod of sound. She said, "Is it time?" Someone off camera said, "In twelve, eleven, ten, nine, eight, seven, six, five, four, three, two, one, now," and the juror crossed the remaining space rapidly. Trembling began to rack her as she got close, but she continued and made it into the chair. She lifted the helmet in her hands and set it on her head and collapsed back, folding her arms over her chest as if in self-protection.

Then it was a still frame, but for the sometime trembling of those protecting arms, a still frame that continued minute after minute. The film blinked out.

"But the rest? What about the rest?"

"That's the film I was to show you. After that, they just go out of the room. The juror goes, the accused goes, the guards go. The accused goes to a holding pen. The guards too. The juror goes to a sitting room and talks with a specialist about what she has seen. Then she formulates her opinion. That ends up being the judgment. It is all very simple. There is nothing in it that you can't do. Each step follows the next."

An insect, some kind of mosquito, was moving in the room and it landed on Marna's neck. She slapped at it and it took off.

"Even here," she said, "in the heart of this place, even here they come after you."

DAY 3

Someone, not Marna, was walking Abel down the hall. It was morning, though no one could see it through the opaque walls of the building. This person was the psychologist. She was introducing herself. She was saying things to him like, I am the psychologist who will speak with you after the repeat room. She was calming him with her ease of manner and practiced air. Abel looked at her distrustfully for the most part and she seemed to feel that.

"I want to know," said Abel, "what it's like in the repeat room for the person who goes in. I haven't met anyone here who has, and no one will say."

The woman adjusted the strap of the bag she was carrying, looking at it for a moment like it was the most important thing in the world. Abel looked at it too. Then the woman looked up at him.

"It isn't that anyone is hiding anything from you. Is that what you think? The accused come out of the repeat room in great confusion. It is a confusing place to be, I think. They remember nothing about what it was like. They have to be told where they are, what day it is. But soon they are back on their feet. Although, of course, not completely, not the ones the judgment goes against. But the others, they leave that very day and go out into the world. And for them the world has changed. It has become a place of promise. No one was ever exonerated so much. It is a kind of miracle that happens here."

They had arrived at a checkpoint. Guards scanned the psychologist's eyes, and scanned Abel's, and they continued on.

"You will have to invent fantasies of secrecy if secrecy is what you want," said the psychologist. "Things here are transparent, utterly transparent. And as for the things you will see when you sit in that chair, well, I'll be there after to help explain them. A lot of work has been done to help explain those things. It is the work done by you and by all your predecessors who have spoken with others like me."

The cross hallways dwindled as they went, and finally they were in a large hallway, somewhat in disrepair. No other hallways crossed it. It turned and

turned again and they reached a medical station outside a set of heavy doors covered in locks.

The psychologist smiled and put one hand on each
of Abel's shoulders, a sort of attenuated embrace.

"I am going now, but I will see you after. You are
not alone in this. You have never been so much a
member of your society."

And then he was in a folding chair, and a man was
taking his vitals. The sound of footsteps came, and
following them was Ludwig. He threw himself into
the seat at Abel's side.

"I hope you slept well."

"A bit. I didn't know there would be someone in
my room."

Ludwig shrugged. "If you had thought about it, I
don't know, perhaps it's obvious."

"Everything looks good," said the tech. "We're on
schedule. Shall I proceed now or . . ."

"There they are," said Ludwig. "Yes, proceed."

"We'll need your arm," said the tech. He took it.
Around Abel's arm he wrapped a rubber cord and
pulled it tight. He stuck a needle into the vein that
was there, and attached it to a bag that hung on a

metal frame. It was all very simple. There was nothing advanced about it, nothing to signal that this was the brightening edge of a new world.

The bag began to drip and its fluid, whatever it was, ran down the line that led to Abel's heart. Up the hallway came guards and those guards were dragging a man by the neck. Their long poles were like the scissors that cut a page in half, or like the legs of swamp birds that stand in water.

Abel saw the accused then as the procession passed and he looked at him. The accused looked nowhere. Nothing he knew could help him then, nothing he saw. His life had gone beyond him. When the door shut, Ludwig touched his watch.

"It begins."

"And now, here, now stand up. You've got it. Stand up."

Abel got to his feet uneasily. His vision resolved. A door was ahead of him, a large door. Someone was opening it. It was open. They led him through. He could walk on his own then, and he did. He entered the room and it was one he had seen before. To his left and right there were monitoring machines of various kinds. Guards were standing there, two of them. They had leaned their poles against the wall and under their hats they were watching him tensely, their flesh pulled back. Abel moved forward and his feet went but these feet of his were slow. It seemed like they were protesting. He made it halfway and halfway and halfway, and then he was there, halfway across the room at this informal line that seemed graven in the ground. He halted and looked back.

"Now," said a voice. "Continue on."

Abel shuddered forward and then he was lumbering on feet that ran beneath him. The room was dusty. It was dirty. As he drew near the hut he saw it was a metal shack. It didn't just look like a shack. It was a shack. His heart was beating with such force you could see it. The repeat room filled his vision. Everything was before him and nothing behind. He was at the chair. He sat in it. He almost collapsed, but lifted the helmet to his head and set it there, set it over his face, and with this gesture, he fell back and into darkness.

A person was like a point of light. A person was standing and the face of the things that faced him were themselves points of light and also planes. They rotated and flashed as they drew near, flashed as they went far. Scale was a disfigured thing, floating deceptively, something in water when you thought it was in air. A figure at dusk that's a bush or a shadow or a figure and it's moving towards you. The scale of what is large goes small. The small contains not smaller things but larger. Turning left turns right. Something was close and it was the wildness of a cheek, of a wet cheek, a child's face, and when it pressed there it was your own face that was pressing. No one could say who he was or she. She was lying in a puddle. She was mud. She had no arms, no hands, no legs. She was he and he was what he saw. A bird went by a window. As simple as that. Someone was looking at a bird and it was impossible. It was a cause for despair. That something could be stuck here, in a room full of toys, stuck in clothing, stuck under sheets and blankets, and the hot air of winter, and there, in the sky, something that was everything you were not. To know you would never be able to get so far from yourself. The bird is gone from the window and the window is not in the wall. Someone sings in the morning and there are boys, hundreds of boys from every direction. They do not dance but it is a dance, a dancing thing, this hundred-headed crowd of boys rioting in their lamplike violent frenzy. A person knows everyone she knows and she thinks of them at once, he thinks of them. He doesn't know who thinks of it, but thinking of it, he is thinking he is one of the boys, a thing that runs in stride in a shape so garrulous and rough, a thing so intricate. An arm is before you when you look and you move it to look at it. You use it to hold things. It is not to be believed, how a thing can move when you tell it to move. And it moves. There were so many wakings, so many fallings into sleep and each momentous as the last, each as strange and long and never as the last. One got used to what could never be gotten used to, and in us-ing oneself suchly one was lost. Falalallalalalalaalla. The edges of things. He held the edge of something

when he did it. What did he do? He did something
and when he did something it was holding the edge
that did it. There was nowhere else to hold and how
could it be? How could you not hold the edges of
things, there was nothing but edges. And then to
turn and look at oneself. To end up partway through
the day in a locker room and voices are calling and
in a mirror, there's your face. It is what it is: not anything you've seen, but all the things you've seen. As
flat and purposeless as a seal's face. Everything turning flat and then receiving shape, then turning flat.
Even the body and the sense of it, it turns flat and we
remember and then we are in it and it has shape and
there is nothing to know that can be known with
shape. Knowing is only flat and being flat is dead. A
wire that ran out the window and squirrels went on
it, running like a road. For years he saw them there
and then they were not there anymore. Some words,
a tree cut down. The squirrels were a tree cut down
and the wire was a tree cut down and the boy watching the wire, seeing the life of the thing, was a tree
cut down. Everything's shadow stretches away from
the observer, a theater of things that can't be seen
because they are in their own depths hiding. I was

working with my hands. Someone had shown me this is the job and how you do it and then I would do it. Hundreds of windows and through the windows were days and through the days hours glittering like rings of necklaces spinning and each wore the head of a workman climbing a ladder. He climbed the ladder to a streetlight and he opened it the same way every time. The same way every time his foot felt the inside of its curve on the steps it went up and the feeling there, that something could be so specific, made a terror in the heart. If there could be one thing that I could see, it must mean I could not see all the other things. I will go into the ground and rot. You were crying as they took you to the nurse and it was not the other boy who did it but you who did it. You had hit him and he had not cried but you had cried. The confusion was enough that the incident vanished. No one spoke of it. He became your best friend. Flailing lines of pavement decline into parts of speech, and ways of saying things one tries to say but can't. Your mother's face is your father's face is a locus of wet things compressing and exploding, pulsing like lungs. You are out of breath on a hill. He is coming up the hill. It is you on the hill. Red and yellow and gray and white things, they have no qualities, only color. What you suspect explodes with nothing because it is filled with nothing but things that might have been but weren't. A flower is ripped in half, but it is plastic and it hurts your hand. It cuts it, and the cut is healed as a scar. Now your hand feels like that, like a hand that did that. And you are that, the thing that did that. The order of it, being young and older, one was younger, was it true? One is older, that is true. One contains the other, but feeling that there were memories, and going into the place of them, and there in the memories, surely he can say, I remember being old, and I know what it was like, and I felt my body breaking when I used it and I woke and I was still young. But no one is there with you when you come out of the bathroom or out of the house and the room or the sky feels impossibly big. You could never cross it. And people watching who you didn't see, thousands of them, who address you only once you move, only once you yourself act. It feels like a race, something that was never begun. And when the light goes out of the sky, there is nothing quiet. Everything in the city creaks, but there is a hush, sometimes, and then the lights go on, all over, like pins. Sitting there on the truck sometimes, and the lights go on, and they say a lamplighter is a city. The people who are old when you were four, where did they go? From beneath the table their faces look at you with pride, and the things they know, you learn mean nothing or less than nothing, they carry them weightlessly into places the subject of which will never be mentioned again. And she is somehow closer than anything can be. She is on the other side of the room and talking to someone and she turns to look and is closer, is made up of things you already know. She is draped with warmth of blankets on the things you know, and her body breaks into song there in your mouth as you look at her glancing at you, and it was the first time you met. She is there in coats in the hallway of a building and she leans into you, and that's it, that's it. The thing could end there, it could. I say that to her, it can end her and we could die today, and she just laughs and pulls me along. The seasons, something that turns like a wheel. But remembering summers are all one summer, all together in a row, they lie. The sand is continuous, one walks from one into the next into the next into the next.

A PERSON WON'T LOOK AT
SOMETHING IT'S THERE BUT I WON'T
LOOK
I WON'T LOOK

Everyone screaming and the heart frightens, but it is joy. They are all smiling and when you look at the smiling you know, the good of it is not anything to be taken away but only felt then, no thing beyond the moment it contains. Or the moment contains the thing the goodness of which is nowhere else and can be nothing else. And all the days walking away over pavement, hands tight in anger in the pockets, mouth working to spit or spitting, muttering, eyes not looking at anything but seeing scenes over and over, scenes replaying, the betrayal of this, the promise of this, the known thing this that was to be mine. I was in love with her and she did not love me. I told him I would stick with him, and there he is and I don't know. The feet strike at the ground in the anger that bristles. Who am I if I am not the things that were done to me? And everyone knows. Everyone remembers everything that was done to me. But small as a tack stuck in a wall, the wall turns and is a floor, and when you are drunk you see, why did I not see like this before? Why do I wait to be like this, seeing things the way they are? And then forgetting and remembering again and forgetting, and the feelings that come in the night, wasn't there more to this? Wasn't I told something, some single fact that, if I could remember it, would show it all up, would show it all as it is, this farce? And then one is oneself and I am speaking to someone in a flower shop and going to a service, or buying any sandwich at all from a man I know, a man I dislike who makes sandwiches. Where in the day is the door to the next day? One is always giving up and going to sleep and then, there it is, the next day, but when did it come? The feeling of everyone knowing more than you, but when you ask them, you can never remember what it was you wanted to know, what it was you thought they knew that you did not.

> A flat image of a room
> and the photograph is black
> a person is standing permanently there
> A flat image of a room
> and the photograph is black
> a person is standing permanently there
> The thing is whirling. The blackness is growing

thicker and thicker. It is in the nose. All the times you almost drowned. You are choking on your own throat. A weakness in the arms. You are on your knees and trying to rise. You are turning over and the smoke is everywhere. There is nothing to see farther than you. A hurt thing cries out, but always it is crying to someone, and so a hurt thing alone cannot cry out, unless it cries out to, it cries out, it cries out to, it cries out to something. A rending and a breaking apart. Something so large it could not possibly fit. It approaches and the senses fail, not fail someone, but fail in themselves, and the moment of it is like the sea being poured out into a, into, something I once saw, I saw.

Abel came to and he was in a chair in a dimly lit room. The front of his shirt was wet with drool. His neck hurt. He tried to sit up and he felt his throat all the way from his mouth to his stomach, to his lungs. He winced.

"Your throat'll feel better soon. We gave you some medicine. You've been vomiting on and off for about four hours."

A man was sitting there, behind the lamp.

"You're okay," the man said. "More than okay. You made it."

Abel looked at him and his vision swam. He leaned back in the chair.

Abel came to again and he was in the same chair. He was in the same room with the same lamp and the same man.

He said, "How long have I been here?"

"It's been eight hours. You're okay. Everything is okay. Just take it easy. Lie back."

"My throat hurts."

Abel sat up. He looked like a fever victim and his hands trembled when he let them go.

"Some water."

"Here you go."

Abel got to his feet uneasily and tried to walk somewhere, but there was nowhere to go. He crossed the room and sat in another chair. As soon as he sat, he seemed to lose his balance and he slumped, but then sat up again.

"Who are you?"

"I'm just here until you need me to go, and then I'll call Alina."

"Alina?"

"She's the doctor you met, the psychologist."

Abel nodded.

"Here's some food for you," the man said. "If you can swallow it, they say, it means you can hold it down. Amazing how the body works."

He put a pan of food on the table. He took the cover off and steam rose.

She had shut the door and she had taken off her coat. She had sat down and she had looked at him. She had set out a device on the table and she had written things in it. She had said her name and she had spoken to him in a manner that made sense, for things that make sense.

Abel sat and looked at her and seemed to be trying to remember.

He was a person with the look of a person remembering.

"When a juror sits here," she said, "the juror feels in their mind all that they saw, feels it at once, and so it's hard to remember it, or to put it in order. And that's why we have developed a system of things. Do you know what a system of things is?"

Abel nodded weakly, but didn't look at her.

"There are different ones. People call them taxono-mies or cosmologies. There are systems of things that vary depending on if the things are real or imagined, if the things are terms that themselves refer to still other things. This system is a system of archetypal situations. Do you know that there are really only so many stories, there are only so many stories that happen in the world? Human beings are repeating the same stories over and over. It's our fate and our life, and it is comforting in a way. One of the things I can do for you to help you organize what you saw is that I can show you the kind of stories, the kind of scenarios that life is made of, and you can put the things you felt in these boxes. When they are there, they resolve into narratives and they can help you know what hap-pened and what it meant. Does that make sense?"

She clenched her hand over a device she held and a whirring sound came. Then a hologram appeared on the table.

"This is a typical scene. I think you know it. Do you know it?"

"Parents fighting."

"That's right, parents fighting. This is one of the central experiences of human life. Here's another."

"Hiding something," he said.

"That's right, the child is hiding something it shouldn't have. Otherwise why would she hide it? Here's another."

"Leaving in the morning?"

"You've got the hang of it now. There are hundreds of these. Leaving someone behind in the morning is one of them. The work we have to do now is to settle on some of these and try to find how what you saw was actually not the chaos it seems, but just a series of these, of these archetypes. And then the creases will unfold, the whole thing will lie flat. We will help you make your decision."

Abel stood in the judgment room. He wore a new set of clothes and they hung on him falsely, obviously clothes that were not his. He stood and the doors opened and the accused was brought in. Abel looked at the accused and saw something, saw his face as if for the first time, perhaps he saw that he was looking at someone who was only a boy, really just that. He took a step towards him, but blunted himself, stepped back and stood impassively. The guards dragged the accused onto the stage, there by the concrete killing chamber. The boy was terrified. He was crying and shaking. They were holding him up by the neck.

Everything was frozen, there, just like that. It was a tableau, an engraving, order and disorder perched on each other's shoulders like ill-fed birds.

Then a voice came from behind, "We record the verdict in case 90134."

Abel had sat down. Somehow he was sitting when he was supposed to be standing. He stood. The space was long before him, but every noise was consequential in a place like that. It was the moment for him to speak. It was like a spotlight was shining on him, but there was no spotlight. He met the eyes of the accused and when he made his judgment he spoke loud so that anyone could hear.

2: RECORD

My sister used to say, let us inhabit the moment of our love, not just now, but for our whole miserable, pitiable lives. And I would listen, as I always listened. Standing, listening, watching. She would tell me things. She'd tell me anything, anything real, anything unreal. She made the world we lived in with her hurried, rapid phrases, so many I can hardly remember them all. Pleas, elaborations, imperatives. Nothing was too much. My father and mother who raised us in that loveless house on a black hill with nothing surrounding it and nothing within, they told us we must be our own resort. You must be your own resort, he said to me, and you the same, to her. My mother said, there isn't anyone who will help you or want to. You must carry your own help like food in a bag. My father hated the way the world had become. He was a romantic. Like all romantics, he loved the past, some past in some way particular to him, and went there to live in his head. From it he drew an awful thing; from it he made the house in which we lived and its rules, rules that marked and drove my life. The first rule, he said, as he said it so often, still each time it was with the emphasis of speaking to one who has never heard, a useful thing for one like me, who indeed never hears, who is, as my father would often say, smiling somewhere else, the first rule, he said, the first rule is, there is no one where you are. You think there is someone there, standing in your skin, but there isn't. Accept it. If you would like for there to be someone where you are, albeit briefly, you must choose who to be and be that person. He had been trained in the theater, had been an actor and a director. My mother had been a director too, and a better one than him, or so she sometimes said. In their dismay at the useless degenerations and contortions of hypermodernity they had, the two of them, gone, so she would often say, my mother, to the black hill, to the house on the black hill, there to make a fate. We lived like an unanswered burning, the evidence of something ending, but there was no one to see. Like the old riddle where nobody meets no one and everybody can see nothing will happen whatever anyone might say, yes, like that. My father, I tell you, was a romantic, and he rejected the technologies of the day. He rejected the schooling that we were obligated by law to have. Neither my sister nor I ever set foot in a school. If we left the house it was only to go short distances, no more than twenty or thirty feet out onto the property. The house was not a house properly for the obvious reason: it was a set, a stage. We were not children for this couple, our parents, because they were not properly our parents. They were directors, and my sister and I, we were actors, although they, the directors, would act alongside us. The first task, the task of our extreme youth, was to learn what they called sullenness and motility. The hundreds of lectures beat it into us. I recall it in a series of flashed blurred images. The place I would sit on the floor listening, so familiar to me, and as familiar to me the corner of the yard visible through the window, the seat of impossible yearning. Sullenness, sullenness, sullenness. On and on my parents would go. Sullenness is the body waiting, being nothing. It has no emotive quality other than the lack of being. A body is present, but contains nothing. Learn to contain nothing. Motility is the body as origin. The body gives rise, first to the promptings of a heart, and then to the actions of that

heart or life. You stir, my mother would say, to something. You never simply stir. But what is it that calls
you? We would be made to sit, these small children
would be made to sit, for hours on cold paving stones
not moving. Alternately we would be made to link
the chains of why and say them. I run across the
room because the curtain trembles and seeing it I
tremble and want to be with it. This I would shout as
I ran to the curtain. You are always wrong, my
mother told me, when you think you know why you
do things. But you should try to know anyway and
you should cry it out in a kind of wealth. My sister
would sometimes run beside me, and we would imi-
tate each other. She would say, I am sitting on the
floor because I am like a hat. And I would say, I am
sitting on the floor because my sister is like a hat and
I want to be one too. Then my mother, You are not
like hats. Hats do not sit but they are put. Have you
been put? And we would run off, shouting something
else, something else we were doing, and we would
shout it running, and again be contradicted. But
what is it you mean? What do you mean by it? When
we were older, when I was eight and my sister ten, we
were given the scripts they had spent that first decade

preparing. These were dossiers, lists, descriptions of characters. Here on this black hill, my father would begin. Here, yes, here, yes, here on this black hill . . . We were so used to these speeches we could concoct them ourselves. Here on this black hill is the last day of the life you have been living, so said my father as he and my mother brought in box after box. Each box had folders and folders. The folders held the selves and versions, all the ones that we might be, were we told to be. It was like this: my father, my mother would say, you, you are Joan F, and you, you are Medellin K. Then we would be the pair of them, those two, and we would know the history they had, how they behaved. Perhaps there was no point to it. Perhaps like anything, it had no real content, only seemed in its winding and unraveling to give a glimpse of meaning. I could only do what I was told and try, and I did, I tried with everything I had, just as my sister did. For years we woke every day desperate to succeed as we had not the day before. But a one like Medellin K: this is how it would go. Perhaps we were sitting in the main room of the house and lunch was soon to come. I, then, would know how to be, what to say, when to say it, because knowing

Medellin, having read the file on Medellin, having seen the example texts, having in some cases watched films of various characters, I would know what it meant to be a person in the world. It is so terribly hard to be oneself. Much easier to have someone else to be, one person here, one person there. A parade of human weakness and joy. Then the creature Medellin K, taking into account the characters of the others, would begin by craft to undermine what these others were saying, slowly introducing a somewhat poisonous dialectic that would culminate in a grievous fight during the lunch meal. I am speaking of a simple family meal. This was the life we lived: nothing was ever simple. Everything was recursive, level on level on level. My mother might be crying, my father punching the door frame, my sister hiding beneath the table. Everything done with a whole heart—to the edge. And Medellin K laughing and laughing at the trouble he'd caused. For this I was not punished. No, no, never punished for such a thing: Had I not done right? At any time they might have given me a different role to play, if they had chosen to. My parents wanted to survive the dramatic situations of life by seeing them as artificial, environments we could create and collapse at any time, predicated not on who we were but on who we chose to represent. Medellin would ruin the dinner, but only because they had invited him. They could have made me play any one of a hundred characters. The pulse of this human work is the pompous strut of a rooster, our mother told us. Only those who take it seriously are prey to it. But such a complicated task as a Medellin K, that was advanced work. At first the characters we were given were simple, just emotions tagged to a vague purpose. Sad-girl-wants-revenge. Boy-sits-on-floor-for-no-reason. Slowly we worked our way up to true characters, each with a past detailed in the pages we were made to read. In our room, in our few moments of ease, my sister and I would lie weary and spent, embracing on the wooden board that was our bed. She was hard and bony. I was too. There was nothing soft in that world. My parents did not even have a bed. For them a bed was a ridiculous object, that we had one was a sign of our childish weakness. They slept in two chairs, which they positioned so the first rays of the morning sun would wake them. We are robots, my father would say, animated by the plants that have learned to draw energy from the sun. Who is it you're being? I asked him once, when he said that to me, that or something like that, and he said, first teacher. Who is second teacher, then? You have known him other times. And third teacher, fourth teacher? You have known them. Each has a different way, different things that must be done. For instance, when your mother hits you she is fourth teacher, and she is right to do it, but wrong to do it. She is inside a character who does wrong. It is not gentle, but it creates a situation, a calamity, out of which real good can come. Or do you think so? How would you dissect it? If she is no longer the one who hit you, but now a different one bringing succor, what then? Can there be real injury without rancor? Can there be succor? I would begin to speak and he would interrupt: Become Frederick T, he would say. Then being Frederick T, I would not say anything, for Frederick T says nothing. He ends up in corners looking at his feet. His history is, he was hurt and doesn't think much of himself. But he is always planning to run away. It is something he does not accomplish, but he is planning it. All of this is in the file. Sometimes we would make errors, though, real errors. We would forget who should be talking or what they would say or how. Something would come from my mouth when it shouldn't. Or my sister would move in some way, respond in some way not in the nature of the character. Esme L does not do that, my mother would shout. And they would take my sister and shock her on the wrist. And she would scream out uselessly. Sometimes we would faint even before being shocked. Even in that case, though, we would not escape punishment. Whenever we came back to ourselves, we would be brought before the others, not cruelly but transparently. Everything hurtful must be seen, my father would say. The whole thing was without malice. It was, my mother said, a training aid. That's what she called the electric shock device, the training aid. It hung on the wall in the kitchen. I don't know where they got such a thing. It must have been designed for animals. No sane person would use it on a child.

At supper one night, my father, as Lyman W, a character we feared, began to insult the Michael B that I was being. The Michael B that I was had not eaten the food Lyman W had prepared, or that my father, whoever he had been while preparing it, had prepared, and now Lyman W was angry that I wouldn't eat. He said, When I was a boy, there were five of us, five boys. We were five boys, said Lyman W. My father was wearing a shirt with a high collar, often the sort of shirt the Lyman Ws of his repertoire would wear. At such times, my mother would bask back as my sister said, describing their stylized comportment. My mother, as Anise C, basked back, as Lyman W, in a high collar, declaimed. He continued: When I was young, I was the middle boy. We were born all of us within four years. My two older brothers, fraternal twins, then me, then my two younger brothers. We were taught to be sharp and to take what we could from the others. You who are dull can't understand the slightest bit of what I mean, you who have at all moments every last thing you could ever need. Do you know what supper was like for us? Do you know? Do you have any guesses? I'll wait to hear. I said I didn't know. Rubina S said she didn't know either. She looked at me as she said it, but there was none of my sister in her at such times. No part of her recognized me, and no part of me her, just as her body, always mine, was nowhere to be found, replaced by this Rubina S body of which I knew nothing. It was not strange. This was something in the nature of the house. What about you? my father continued. Anise, what about you? My mother kept silent. She didn't even look at him. What supper was like for us, it was like, it was, said my father, as Lyman, speaking of his father, so he said, my father would sit at the supper table, a place to which we, the boys, were never allowed to go, at which we could not sit, although I did at times sneak there in the nighttime and sit just to feel what it felt, so he told us. My father, said my father, in the role of Lyman W, would sit at the table and eat the meal my mother had prepared. As simple as that. She would prepare an enormous amount of food for him, a real feast, something like no one had ever seen, but it would be every night, and he would eat most of it. We would be there at the corners of the room watching him, desperately hungry ourselves. We would get nothing all day. Nothing in the morning. Nothing at noon but what we could find in other people's homes, or steal from shops. Then we'd be faced with the prospect of my father's feast. I don't know that my mother could cook well at all, but we thought the food she made was the finest food there was and we longed for it. We would crouch there, under the table, or under the adjacent furniture, watching, hoping that my father, on this day, was not hungry, or not hungry enough to eat it all. Is there a limit to hope like that? Mine was endless like a banner. And all the while the sound of his mouth and teeth and tongue. Time would pass, the noise of eating would cease. My legs and arms would tense. You would hear the chair creak, and then he would set the serving plate down on the floor, and the five of us, flying suddenly from who knows where, would be at it, pushing, clawing, punching each other. I might get a big gob or morsel and make away with it to the wall, where my larger brothers would catch me, and take it away. Or my smaller brothers might find some good part of the plate, some part with plenty on it, and think they could have it, and I would get down on them and get their neck in my hands and pull them to where I could eat the thing they wanted, the thing they had had. Do you know what food is? That's what food was, that's what supper was for me. Never enough. And you, here you are, with your own plate. I mean, look at it. Look at it in all its beauty. A real plate, do you perceive it? It's right there. That plate isn't Rubina's plate. It isn't my plate. Michael, it's your plate. You're in no danger of having it taken. No one is going to pick it up like this and throw it. He picked up my plate then and cast it across the room, where it shattered. He pointed his face at me in that so-soft affection of cruelty. Michael, Michael . . .

Now that it's happened, how do you like it? I flinched back in my chair with an ashen frozen mouth. No one, he said, continuing, does anything with your plate, or with your allotted portion. If there's any danger, he said, coming around the table, it's that someone will shove your portion down your throat, like this. He grabbed me and started to shove the meat of a duck into the hole of my mouth, pushing it past my teeth. I went limp. I must confess, I was too afraid to bite him.

As time passed and we grew fluent in the characters, we began to invent characters of our own and present them to our parents. Such a thing was allowed, even celebrated, though my parents would edit the files, subtract traits, add others, change the histories ever so little. They wanted to be sure we were not trying to construct a self. So I could make a character if I liked, and did. But what was not celebrated was divergence. We would be punished for diversion even, or I should say, especially, from a character or script we had ourselves prepared. Was it fair? Would my parents be likewise punished for mistakes? It is impossible to say because never once did I or my sister observe my parents make a mistake of any kind. They had trained their whole lives for this peculiar effort, the raising of us and the making of our scripts, and they had been hurt and punished their whole lives, which was the cause of this peculiar effort, the raising of us and the making of our scripts. It is nonsense, my father would say, to believe you can be a person. You cannot be a person. You can wear a person on you, drape it over you. Expecting to be someone leads to melancholy, leads to the inured semi-death of the heart. Rather, be, riotously, one, then another, then another. Be Argus F now, come on. Be Argus. I will be Santander S. A shifting of appearance, gait, mien. Then they would come together in that room, two who we knew so well, to speak and behave and perform the actions of people, the persons Santander and Argus. But were we burdened by a son and a father at such times? Were we prevented by our blood from being strangers suddenly, as if a door were thrown open, so suddenly? Not that I remember. Once I, as a bellicose man of fifty, slapped my father for making a joke at my expense, and he took it. He did not even appear surprised. Because it was script-appropriate it was acceptable to our elders, though no one showed delight, of course. The blow occasioned no schism, no further trouble. I suppose the way the roles were written, it was rarely possible for such a thing to occur, my sister and I were somehow always naturally subordinate, naturally what you might call grovelers, followers, petitioners, but once or twice it did happen. Ten minutes later, my mother was reading aloud to the three of us as we sat on the kitchen floor and we were all as unalarmed as any four could be.

Still, we, my sister and I, in the quiet of our room would leave the permissions of the family, and wonder what else there was. There we came up with other characters, ones of which we would never speak to our parents, ones we might be only each for the other. These we did not write down, but spoke into friendly ears in the smallest moments of the night. This was the way it began. Take your clothes off, she'd say. You don't need them with me. And I would take my clothes off. She would take hers off too, removing these useless and often disgusting objects of cruelty and status, and when she had removed them I knew her better, every inch of her. I would go on my back and she would climb naked over me, my dear sister. She would put me in her as easily as anyone might, this creature, this human animal, and move above me, and I would grab at her with my hands, trying to get as much of it as I could, as much of her as she leaned above me in the day or night. Like beasts we were seldom given the actual reasons for things and so our existence wasn't troubled by continuity. My sister was fourteen or fifteen and she began to whisper to me the nature of a person who I ought to be for her, a nameless character. She said, and this is what he does, and this is what he has done to him, and she began to do it, and I began to do it, too. I did not feel guilty or awful. I felt no wrong, but only the outline of her shape and mine, and the wet confusion of animals, the wetness of the inside of animals and of the confusion of inside for outside. Her tongue was in my mouth and on my teeth and mine moved over her face. I licked her wherever I could. Like a dog I tasted her asshole and licked it and kissed it. I licked her legs and her stomach and her feet. She held her balled-up sweater over her mouth so her cries wouldn't be heard, and when it was my turn to shout noise, she held the sweater over me. I thought I would die. Then we would be there, beneath a ceiling in a silent room, our chests heaving. This was what a sister was for me. I put everything into her, all I could feel or know. In our studies, we would get to be in the various modes, but never choose. We were not unacquainted with shame and horror, sadness. These were our daily friends, just as joy, gratefulness, impetuous bravery, all came and went. Alaina G was a face of shame my sister would be called upon to wear, a person who had never been more wrong than then, who was always in the worst moment of her life, knowing worse things she could not disclose to those people who, looking upon her, thought her the vilest of any creature. Be Alaina G, my father would say, and my sister would grovel, or piss herself, right there in the room. I couldn't sit by her then, because there was no character I had who would, no one so lowly, though I had dozens and dozens of characters, male and female, just as she did. When we would get too used to a role, my parents would sometimes withdraw it. You are now attempting to penetrate the role, et cetera, et cetera, to put more there than was there to begin with. It can serve you no more. And so we would move on. My mother would always be the first to spot this. She took notes on a tiny pad of paper and kept them collated in a kind of larger register in a room at the back of the house. I am tracking your progress, she would say. This, then, is the document of your progress. Whose progress? I would say, and she would laugh. No one's, no one's. To obtain food, my father and mother sold two-minute dramatic scripts to advertising concerns. This they freely confided. My father would go to town once a month, receive the correspondence, make his replies, and return. He would bring back food, clothing, whatever we needed. When he was leaving he would stop at the door and say the same thing, always the same thing: if you run away, your sister will be beaten to death. Or, if you run away, we will strangle your brother in a bag. The two of you are useful, interesting only together. There would be no reason to keep only one of you. We believed him completely. I know that he meant it. I know too that he was not cruel, neither he nor my mother felt anything like cruelty. Rather they were performing a precise experiment. They had a thing they needed to do and we were the doing of it. For it they needed us both and they needed our absolute participation. For years they had it, and in a way, you could say, they still have mine. For I am still alive. My life is made in the direction they indicated at some point in the past on a piece of lined paper. What would a son be like? Could we have such a son? they must have said. A child made the way a character is written. What would a character be like? It began as a sheet. I would be given a sheet. Perhaps at the top it would say the name: Albinez O. Then it would say the age of the person, thirty-nine years of age. Albinez O, thirty-nine years of age, prematurely white hair, slight facial tic. A drinker. Sadness b/c of partner's death (cancer). Middle child. Parents mild, useless people of ordinary wealth. Owns cats. Spends evenings in local bar. Works as a guard at a hospital. Often overcleans his uniform and overprepares it, lays it out on an unused bed in the house. Most important person in his life: his superior at the hospital, a woman named Jeri. He is afraid of her. Commonly jocular with other low-status men. Will tell jokes at such times. Around high-status men, women, completely silent. Around low-status women feels violence but does nothing. Then there would be sample dialogues to memorize and extrapolate from. Sometimes a level of diction specified, but more often simply implied by the character study. Of course there were characters we did not want to be. My father would say, Be Malena N, and my sister would practically groan. If she did groan, she would be shocked for showing a nature. You have no nature, they would tell her, and she would be brought to the kitchen and shocked with the training aid. Show no nature. Then she would have to be Malena N for a whole day. She would have to wear Malena N like a paper bag over her head. I think sometimes my parents would use us as punishment too. They would pick some role for me that would make it worse for her, say, Stepanek T. Stepanek T was always trying to get my mother to hold his hand or sit with him. He was obsessed with the set of characters my mother would play, and depending on who she was, would chase her around relentlessly, seeking affection. He was pathetic, just the worst of the ones I had to play, save perhaps for

Carol Y, who had been my favorite, but who my parents altered as a punishment, one of the great disappointments of my childhood. In any case, Stepanek T would be chasing my mother around, petting her, trying to curry favor. Of course, my mother would not allow any real physical affection to take place. The scripts had been made to prevent it, but still there my sister would be, Malena N, by the window, just crying and crying, and she would have to look over and see me, the one she loved, running after our mother like a kid goat. Though I don't know what it was my parents knew. I don't know that they knew we felt any sentiment for each other whatsoever. It seemed sometimes neither of them were or ever had been capable of sentiment. And if that were true, why would I expect them to believe others capable of it?

My sister ran about the house, as you know, in these threadbare, badly sewn garments (just as I did), and as she got older, she grew more and more pronouncedly female. I suppose it is a thing that happens. In my jealousy, I worried that my father would begin to take her, or to do things to her. This never came to pass. In some character, my sister would be agonizing on the floor over some misapprehension or misdeed, in some complicated articulation of one role or another, one speech or another, and her shirt or dress would be half undone, practically falling from her. I would be hard put, in the role I had, to not feel what one might feel at such at time, and I wondered what my father felt, looking down at this self-entranced languid girl groveling in her shape. It is hard to say whether her performances constituted naivety or simply the correct manipulation of bystanders using the tools at her disposal. She was smarter than I was, and older, so I expect anything I might have known, anything I know now, she knew more. In any case, she was not fondled or raped, and neither was I. Our parents were always more apt to shock us than to speak to us or hit us. They were reluctant to touch us; the reason I think was that we disgusted them. We were so much smaller, and malformed; even when we reached our full growth we weren't as large as they were, the proper size for a person. Our weakness perhaps was disgusting. In any case we were not penalized for that. When the punishment came, the reason was always the same. Every infraction was the same. We could not break character. It was the only real wrong of the house. When my father took me up and stuffed the food in my mouth for not eating, there had been no crime in not eating. He was simply elaborating Lyman W, who hated my not-eating. It was all in the dossier. As Michael B I could well have done something to avoid or object to the punishment, and I would not have been further punished for such an objection. It would have been intrinsic to the scene. But I, as Michael B, had been petrified. I had lost all my resources. Perhaps had I been someone else at the moment, I might have eluded him, gone under the table, for instance, as I had done in earlier times, or called for Rubina S to help me flee, begged for mercy at the feet of Anise C. What he would have done, I don't know. But for such a behavior I would not have been shocked.

What my sister saw when she looked at me, I don't know. I expect she thought of us as being much the same thing, simply the same thing sparked twice by some like circumstance. Anyone would do, she said to me once, for instance, being here in my place or your place, as you, as me, anyone would do as well, would function as easily, because whoever it would be would have had the same beginning as we had, would be the same, would be as well you, as well me. Humans replace one another without apparent effort, for in that situation in which they are, the total situation, they must be the same. They are helpless not to be. This thing that looks out my eyes is the same that looks out yours, only its circumstance is varied. Do you know what it is varied by? One year, eleven months, three days. That I am female is meaningless to me. When she said this, I thought what I always thought, which was, this thing that she thinks is something I think. I don't need to think it because she has thought it for me, and now I have it, and having it my life is richer. Seldom can I remember flinching from her in hurt. But those times were all of a piece, in a single season, and they were in the house, in the public space of the house, and there at those times she was every time Natalie E, a person to whom I owed only pain and shame. This was when I was fourteen. I had been acting out again and again. My father even moved the training aid into the living room, to be closer, for we spent more time there, so often did he administer it to me. I began to have seizures even on days when I was not shocked, and would go through glassy periods, what I called, what I and my sister called glassy periods, in which I would sit and stare and say nothing. My mother realized they had to stop shocking me, at least for a while, and so they introduced a new measure, Natalie E, a kind of enemy. I did not ever see her dossier, and the subject of Natalie E was so painful to me that I could not and did not ever speak about her to my sister, but I can imagine that the dossier compelled my sister, in the role of Natalie E, to every conceivable meanness, smallness, viciousness. Whoever we were being, whatever we were about, in the midst of one or another script, if I displeased, we would hear, EYES DOWN. Then: Natalie E, Roger Q. Begin. And Natalie would lace into me with the most incredible cruelty and ridicule. I was cowed before her, always cowed, capable of no resistance. Even when I was given a character who could resist and should, I would be cowed, and then I would be not only mistreated in my character, but beaten in my physical person. Finally, some weeks after Natalie E was brought out, my sister conducted her only act of disobedience. Anytime they made her Natalie E, she faced the wall and did nothing. This ended Natalie

E, the only time we successfully called for the end to a role or scene.

For with the roles, we never got to say when they began or ended. This my parents did. But in our room alone we could and did, delightedly. I would specify for my sister and she for me. Be Constance, be Chloe, be Philip, Jaime, Sume . . . But we could break when we liked, if we felt that we wanted to, though of course we were gentle to take into account the other's intent in asking us, in setting us into the character in question. One wanted always, I wanted always to be the blank space in which my sister could occur. Somehow the nature of forbidding was not evident in us. There was nothing forbidden and nothing deserved. My sister never felt we deserved any good or any bad, and I neither. Only in our characters did we learn of these things, and to be truthful, we found it hard to understand. Even wanting was hard. We had to learn, we had to teach each other what wanting to meant. This was something we didn't know for a long time. I never knew who I was being when I was between characters. For that we had to invent new characters. We had too long outgrown our selves, whatever they had been, for we'd had them too briefly in our spates of motility-training to be them with any accuracy, and could speak only through these kaleidoscopes of narrative shape. When my sister would lie on me on the floor of our room, she would be any of a number of people, and as each she would behave differently.

Pleasing her, I would be many different people. As these different people, I would treat her gently, kindly, cruelly, brutally, or any combination according to our rules. There were two lovers, Lis and Barry, who had a pact. They would injure themselves, each one injuring itself on behalf of the other and on behalf of itself, as a testament to the love they had for each other. These injuries were made on the inner arm where they would not be seen. I am certain my parents saw them in the course of time, but perhaps they thought these wounds part of the price of the thing. That must have been how it was for them. For us the wounds were a kind of record of time in that timeless place, and also something we could have, for we had so little. We did not know how to have things, even, and so our wounds were a lesson in having. What possessions did I have? They were: a few sets of clothes, a toothbrush, the files (which were not properly ours, which were always being taken away). Everything else we would have to borrow from my parents: books, paper, pencil, whatever we might use. We would have to ask if we could borrow it, and often we were not allowed. Asking for anything was difficult and confusing—for who was asking and why? Therefore having for us became what we could know together, what we could agree was real and would remain real.

EYES DOWN, my mother would shout. EYES DOWN, my mother seemed always to be shouting or about to shout, and we froze, or would freeze, or would imagine freezing, trembling. In our trembling, we desperately froze, and filled our eyes with the floor, with our feet, with the legs of chairs. One minute, two minutes, three minutes. An hour might pass and we could hear our parents going about their business. Get to your room, they'd finally say, as if they were speaking to someone else, to people we didn't know.

We were never worried that my sister would become pregnant because my parents had had us operated on, both of us, so that we were sterilized. So we were told. The operations took place, a doctor came to the house (where they got such a person, who can say), the operations happened, right there in the kitchen, and then when we woke up we were told what it had been, though, of course, I don't know what was done to me. This was a kind of therapy, so my mother told us. You have been sterilized as a kind of help. The march of humans through the world and the centuries, millennia, et cetera, has created habits based on your hope for the so-called passing-on of your genes. The therapy we give you is this: you will not engage in the passing-on of your genes. Therefore you can freely discard those behaviors pertinent to the general mass of gene-passers trying to grub their genes on to others who should not ever even have been given life but unfortunately will be, and for whom life will be, as it is for nearly all, a terrible curse rather than any manner whatsoever of given good. Unfortunately all these grasping groping humans will bear litters of piglets from now until kingdom come, each litter more idiotic than the one before. So my mother would say, going on and on. One had the sense she had not wanted, herself, to have children. It was a sacrifice she had made, a sacrifice punctuated by our sterility. All this to say:

I lay with my sister thousands of times, slept with my penis half inside her many of the nights of my life, and she did not become pregnant because her insides were not functional for the future generations of man, just as my penis and testicles were denuded of hereditary utility, cleaned out like a fish is cleaned before cooking. They were functional enough for our delights, though, and for our delights we used them. I don't know that we ever spoke about the lack of issue, or our prospects as issueless humans. When I think about the list of things we never spoke about, I am troubled to account for it. I can only say that although it seems that in childhood there is endless time for everything, in fact there is only enough of time for a tiny set of things to occur, and that those things happening, one after another, to a person or to persons not cognizant of the incredible brevity of the event, the things happen at times as if to one who is asleep. Only after do we wake and wonder—how could I have never said this, or known that. What did I give up unknowingly? So often it seems there was a place adjacent to the one in which we were— and yet we never went there. It would have been the work of a moment to do so. But it never happened and now it never can.

One of my sister's characters, Grace L, would hurt animals. I did not ever see her do it, because we had no animals, but she was always talking about it, Grace L, with great animation and energy of delight, and it was a struggle for me, if I was supposed to be a like-minded character, to not vomit, so explicit were her illustrations of the brutality she imagined herself perpetrating on some cat or rabbit or puppy. My mother would be taking notes. My father would sit cross-legged, encouraging the dramatization or even participating. Then, if I would break character and vomit, I would be taken and dashed to the ground and my mother would hold the shocking stick and it would be pressed to my wrist and I would cry out and all the while my sister could not stop what she was doing, but would be required to continue on and on, saying, And the rabbit will be pinned beneath the leg of a chair and I will sit my weight down on the chair, and feel through the chair the softness of the rabbit, and feel it too in the noises the rabbit makes, the cries that it gives as it attempts to convince me, its captor, that it should be allowed to go, or if not me, the cries that it makes to the world to allow it to stop being a rabbit, this ridiculous assemblage of fur and bones and blood. Please, the rabbit seems to say, end me and let me be something else. And I would be crying in pain from the training aid. I wondered each time how it could be that she could speak so convincingly about the harm she would do to the rabbit or the cat or dog or bird, whatever it was. I wondered that, but wondering, I knew how it was: her affection for things, something natural to her, was her guide to its opposite. It was because she so wanted to be a bird or a cat or a rabbit, to touch one, that she could speak of the harm done to it. Or else it was simply that she herself had been hurt so often she knew better than anyone how to explain such hurt, how to eke it out slowly but visibly like drops from a dropper, so it could be known in all its excruciating limitlessness.

She would say to me, sometimes, as we lay on the floor of our room, Which one, and I would say, One, and then she, being that one, would say something like, it was always different, but it was always something like, There is a boat, and the boat is traveling on a canal. Wherever they want they can stop the boat. Where do they want to stop the boat? And I would say, Who should answer? And she would say one of the names, and I would answer, I would say, something like, it was different every time, but something like, They stop the boat at a town, but the town is empty. Where have the people gone? she would say. No one knows where the people have gone, but we can go into any house. Any of the houses—all the doors are open. And we would go into one of the houses, perhaps a tall house drawn like a castle, or a house you might see in an old photograph, or a house such as would be modeled in miniature, a house into which anyone who saw it must need completely, totally need to enter, we would enter it and there would be things inside, the belongings of people, the evidence of lives, evidence of every kind, all the evidence that we had not been allowed to be acquainted with, there it would be, laid out like suits of clothing, and we could put them on and speak of them and revel in them, running from house to house, riding the boat from town to town without end. And what would you do with me in a place like that? my sister would say. I would wrap you in a blanket and make you tea. I would dig a hole and bury you in it to your neck. I would breathe in from my mouth through your mouth until your lungs burst and then I would have you. And then I would have you, she'd say. I'd say it, she'd say it. And then I would have you.

We woke up together every day, my sister and I, at the same moment. Until she was gone, I had never woken up and not seen that she was beside me, opening her eyes identically, although, of course, for her there were the years when I was not yet born. She described to me my arrival into the house as the greatest event of her life. Many children, so she told me, fear the advent of a new child in the life of the family, but for her it seemed that there was no family, no life, during these first two years, until I arrived, or so she described it to me. It was as if the family had been paused, set at a standstill, until it could begin full-made with all four participants. How could it be, I asked her, that you could remember what it was like to be alive when you were two years old? I don't doubt you, I told her, but it is not easy to believe. I remember my whole life, my sister said, or would say, I remember it all, even being in the womb. I remember the different light where the world was, on the other side of my mother's skin, and I remember arriving there, in that great bloody cough. My parents did not hear her say these things because they did not allow us to speak about the time before we took on roles. That time was necessary, they would say, but it was a sullen time. It is the origin of nothing now. All things through the whispering voices you assume. Apart from the characters there were dialogues too—set pieces to memorize entire. We would know them backwards and forwards and be asked to speak either side. For instance, one would say, At that time, I was a young doctor, and the nurses would make fun of me. Then the other would say, I don't believe it. Make fun of you. Yes, make fun of me. How would they make fun of you? They would hide my tools inside the cavity of the body I was working on whenever I turned my back. They would pretend to get phone calls from people I knew at crucial times in the operation. Your wife is going into labor, they would say. I don't even have a wife! I would shout back. These were the sorts of routines, and there were hundreds of them. You would know that you should speak one side because someone had spoken the other. You would always be on your guard, always ready to hear these spurring words. And sometimes you yourself would be the lead-in. Sometimes it would be for you to begin such a thing. There were set pieces that lasted a moment, some that lasted minutes or an hour, even a few which went for hours, with a great deal of specified action. I am speaking about something like to a full-length play, but which one is required to be prepared to perform at all times using whichever character one happens to be. And if one fails in this, the punishments begin. Some set pieces were like pageants that would occur seasonally. Others were occasioned by wordplays or jokes my mother or father would make. We were always trying, my sister and I, to detect the rationale behind the chain of events you could call our childhood, but perhaps it was as our parents so often said: there is no reason for anything. No reason, no purpose, no meaning. My parents so often made their sentiments clear: We are having a game in which two full-size organisms have made two new organisms and are trying, within the framework and without the framework of a failed culture, to create a circumstance of freedom from personality for the pair of young organisms, a thing the older organisms can never have, but wish they could, this wishing even being the thing that they would like to avoid, since wishing is at its heart a kind of immense shame. It was so hard to understand what our parents meant by what they did. In the end, we could do nothing to try to please them, because we could not really guess who they were. There was only the endless succession of sketches, one after another, after another, the endless declaration of roles, so many of which I didn't even want to take part in. Even sickness was no safety. We would be put on a stack of blankets in the common area, and made to carry on as invalid versions of whatever character we had been told to be. In particular, I remember my sister in the role of Jack M, sick and vomiting, and being made to follow script by my mother, even as my father held the bucket into which this Jack M vomited.

There were, I should mention, emergency words that our parents might use to signal the end of a charade. We were not to use those words, my sister and I, because we could not possibly have occasion to use them. But our parents, who provided for us, and who were, despite their participation in the life we lived, living another life as well, one in which they dealt with the exigencies of the outer world, did sometimes need to call a halt to our endless play. Then my mother might say, Eyes down. We would immediately stop all action and stand, looking down at our feet, saying nothing, for whatever duration, sometimes an hour or more. If I, in the mode of a disobedient character, failed to adhere to this, as I did upon several occasions, I was shocked not once but several times, invariably leading to a fit of fainting which would occur not only during the shocking, but at intervals thereafter, sometimes for the day or two following. Any such rebellious behavior on my part was celebrated by my sister in private, though I cannot recall a single instance in which she actively strove against my parents and their designs. What did we wear? A series of dully colored garments sewn by my parents. For my sister, there were pants and shirts but also sometimes dresses. Until I was fifteen and outgrew her I wore her previous clothes, many of which, to me, carried some psychic stink, some agglomeration of contact with this body that I loved.

My sister was not attractive, not like those people in the films that I have seen who others want, people sought after as possessions. Her features were not quite symmetrical and she went about rather gracelessly. Perhaps this was a result of the repeated use of the training aid or malnutrition. Who can say? I have had the same treatment she had, and likely with the same result. In any case, what I saw in my sister was something plastic, something that could both alter and stay, and I thought of her ceaselessly. She was like a constant obeisance, an endless praying that my lips could do even as they did the rest, a kind of demented eidetic muttering that came always out of the corner of my mouth. At all times I knew her location in the house and what she was doing. There was no part of her that was unfamiliar to me, just as I was completely bared to her. There was no question of whether I liked her or she liked me. We were simply two parts of a thing that locked together. We had no solace but in each other. Even when she wore costumes, which we did at times, she could not be disguised from me. I felt I could see her through walls. We were so rarely let outside that we owned no shoes. Instead we had thick socks with coarse cross stitching on the bottoms to help grip the floors. I loved to hold my sister's slender legs bare at the thigh where her socks ended and feel my skin against her, to tug and turn there in her grip, to turn her there in my grip, to be gripped and gripping turn her in my ecstasy the shallowness of which was everywhere, was not a thing in particular, but the surface of all things. She was always stronger than me, for my curiosity was this: What would she do? I was always more interested in what she would do than in what I myself might have occasion to do, and so, between us, all the strength was hers; she was the origin of whatever we did. My mother and father would drink sometimes at night, and we were banned to go near. Perhaps this was their weakness, their failure. Or it could simply have been another of their designs. I have never been

in any position to judge them. You may not enter
this part of the house, this much we were told. Then,
at the very edge of this-part-of-the-house we would
crouch and listen. We would hear them at distance,
arguing, carrying on, or even having sex themselves,
or what sounded like sex. We were curious about
this, were curious about everything that was hidden,
but we knew completely how easy they would find it
to kill us if they chose. On many occasions indeed
they came close. We were always in their power, if
for no other reason than that we knew nothing at all
about the world. In fact, I still know nothing about
the world. They knew this, felt sure of our pathetic
weakness and dependence, and relying on it, would
test us. If someone came to the door, my sister and I
would be given hurried roles and sent by ourselves to
greet them. It was, as I say, a kind of test, for I suppose
there was some tiny chance we might have spewed
some wild tale and begged the neighbor to save us,
but I do not think we could have even comprehended
what it would have meant, to be saved, nor known
that being saved might be a preferable condition to
that species of being in which we labored. In any case,
there we would be at the open door. Our neighbors

were not nearby, and were few, but occasionally had reason to come, perhaps to borrow something. It was something like: Oh, hello, Mrs. Edriksen. How are you today? Yes, we are fine, fine, as you can see. Still growing! Yes. Some eggs, is that what you want? Ah, and here is our dish from last time you are returning. I think we have one of yours. We will fetch it for you from the kitchen, and the eggs, of course. Do wait here, or come in. Will you come in? No, of course, of course. I'll be only a moment. And my mother, in the space above, watching, taking notes, the results of which we were not given. One of them, the father, the mother would always be lecturing on: what we should know what we must know what we should know what we must know. Often that what was a screed about a society in which we had little part, with which we could not much identify. My mother would be red in the face, in the role of first or second teacher, declaiming: Modernity created a pressure on the individual! It was based on industry. The collectivization of industry, and the shattering of communities. For a long time people had managed to be, not themselves, but their communities. These were ignorant, often brutal communities, but they were communities. Somehow, in the instantization of generalities, in the paying-out of the line of mass-made objects, the individual was created as an obtainer of said same objects. Such an individual had never existed until she was needed to be the obtainer of the things then made. Suddenly that was all she could be. So much for modernity, so said my father, so said my mother. And hypermodernity . . . Hypermodernity creates the individual as a consumer of her own spectacle, that spectacle being a sub-echo of spectacles she herself observes in others' posturing. The weight to create this ever-ongoing echo is complete. She has no purpose but to posture that she is leading a life that originates meaning, when in fact, there is no meaning. Her individuality never existed, and it is impossible for her to take on roles because her own role as arbiter of her social position (a constant ongoing arbitration) takes up the exact space of her life, leaving no room for archetypal roles or meaning outside of the posturing for the signs and signifiers of said roles, said meaning. Our parents would become angry as they told us this. You are lucky to be the opposite. You are devices set in motion to have no signification outside of being the roles you are doing.

Your aspiration should be that of a stone, a plant, a housefly. Your comfort is in knowing your business, in that, in being the knowing of your business, the long extravagant outlay of that. Who is it now that listens to this? Many times he would give this speech, beginning when we could not understand it, and continuing when we heard it as something on lips at the edge of sight, and ending when we knew it so well, it was as though we ourselves were speaking it. For such a thing there is never a possibility of disputation. Our agreement with our father was at the core, like bones in my hand. Never mind that this philosophy, perhaps excruciating in its beauty, seemed in some way to have gone awry, to not be applied in its true state by the people, my father, my mother, in the act of their various hundredfold roles and their sovereignty over us, their children in our acts of our various hundredfold roles and in our failed and refailed failed and refailed displays of inscrutable and indefensible independent character which ever and always led nowhere.

My mother and father, in various characters, would argue in the evening time many points of great curiosity. My mother would say, for instance, we should go to the city and live. What we are doing is entirely wrong. Then my father would explain what it was that was ongoing in the city, how even they, the mother and father and two children who lived on the black hill, were participating in the general ugliness of the city by earning wealth through the sale of advertising (a great irony), and that this very advertising diminished the intellectual capacity of the city-dwellers, making it even less likely that they, the mother and father and two children, could happily participate in that society at any time in the future. Or my father would have the character who wanted to leave, and my mother its opposite, and he would say, But there are trains that go the length of the country. We could ride on those trains together, give up everything and just go. We could even leave these children behind. Who cares what would happen to them? They are old enough to fend for themselves. At some point this farce must come to an end. Why not now? Tonight? And my mother would laugh and play with her hands and say, I do, like a daring and devil-may-care man, but, darling, all places are the same. There's nowhere we could reach on a train that would be any different from here. The world isn't flat. It doesn't pour over its edge into some other, truly other, place. It circles about. The cat bites its tail. We would take the train only to end up somewhere like this, worse than this, probably, and having to begin again. Or she might even say, What did taking the train do for us the last time? We left behind two children then, and had to start again from the beginning. You didn't have to bear two new children, did you? That was for me to do. I don't want to do that again. I don't even know if I could. Perhaps these little shits have rendered me barren. We might just be stuck here with them for the rest of our lives. My sister and I would watch this sparring with great pleasure. The depth of their roles was a puzzle. My father would say, Depth comes not from calling forth the life you have and know, but from reaching through the character to a life you do not know. The effort to be a person is a wasted effort. Instead be the dragged litter, the litter that carries a pile of skulls, in each the dust of a different life lived entirely. But though there was room for them to teach us, there was never room for us to ask about what we were taught, not really. Who did you want me to be? my sister once asked my mother. Such a simple thing, but to ask it required an infinity of cunning. It was concealed in a role, a person in the play we were performing speaking to the metafictional director, the role my mother at that moment was playing, but of course, it was as well the thing said from the daughter to the mother in the envelope of our actual life. My mother did not falter: for them the philosophy was total. She had given up any aspiration for continuity. What she could be she could be only in a role. She had no opinions or thoughts as such, and my father neither. Only by being father-as-character, by being mother-as-character, could they speak.

That last day the sheet was tangled on my leg as if in some trivially measured prophecy. I opened my eyes and there beside me her eyes opened. We stretched and sat and found again that we were alive. This was a week in which my parents were pushing us, a birthday week, the week of my sister's birthday, notable not as a thing intrinsic to her, but a thing intrinsic to the experiment upon which we were embarked. It was the anniversary of the beginning of the experiment, a beginning which of course was partial, since the full beginning came only at my birth. Still the births were linked, joined together by an integument: what my mother could bear. She bore my sister, and then, as soon as she could bear to, she bore me also, and, as we were told upon occasion, this bearing was nearly the death of her. I do not believe it, for the reason that my mother was a large and powerful woman. In some sense it seems certain that my sister and I were spat out of her vagina without apparent effort. Still, she would harp on what she had done, when in the particular role: aggrieved mother, a role which, to be sure, she rarely played. The birthday week was a kind of metrical moment, a sort of processing. We had had many roles taken away. We were given a set of harsh, difficult roles, roles to judge progress. Roles to be played on hands and knees, you could say, roles to be played through a blurred squint. My sister and I generally hated this time, though in no way did we ever show it. The ways in which we could call for love were so few. Out in the house I felt I was caught in the open. Even the apparent possession of any continuous I would lead to immediate discipline. So sometimes at the door that led out of our room I felt a slight hesitation. Who was I to be?

Every day it was the same. My sister and I would go out of the room and shut the door behind us. There was a taped line on the floor of the hall there, and we would stand beside each other on the taped line and wait for our parents to come. Some time would pass and we would hear them moving towards us. They would arrive and say the names of the characters we were to be. Then we would stand swaying a while longer, recalling what needed to be recalled. Meanwhile they would go back about the house, beginning the tasks of the day. When we went to join them we could go as who we were, who we had not known we were even a moment before. If you had asked me to go into the house and simply do things, I would not have known how. I would have stumbled about trembling in some extreme extension of a constant flinch. Even to begin with, even lying on the bed, eyes open, I would elect, elect at that moment who would do what. I would think, I am Ciara M. Then it was, as it was that day, Ciara M who sat up and looked down at my sister there. I pulled the sheet down from her. Her gray eyes were staring up at me unmoving. I could not tell who she was being. I ran my hand over her, found her breast, and stroked it. Still her eye unmoving. I reached down and pulled her shirt up, moved, and put her nipple in my mouth. Now she made some noise, some trivial sound like something moving in another room, that's what came from her mouth. Giovanna made noises like that, I recall, and bit and scratched. I pulled at her shirt. She pulled her shirt off entirely and I went to her legs and licked and bit them, and pulled them apart. My sister was in a daze from sleeping, it seemed, she was pliable. Are you ready, I said. Who's ready? she said. She tilted her body under me and her breasts became somehow even more evident to me. I pressed against them, trying to feel the whole of her with the whole me, and then we were pushing together, pushed together. She bit my neck and I cried out, louder than I should, but we did not halt. We were growing incautious. We had been kept too long. From the hall we heard steps. Up then we had to go, up and in our clothes and to the line, I shedding Ciara, shedding my sister's body. She shed Giovanna, and then we were in the hall.

You are Goran V, you, Constance C. So said my father. A moment had passed and we were on the far side of the world, there in the house, with his yellowed and incoherent face posing its puzzles to us in the dim light. Goran V, Constance C, okay, never mind that I was covered in my sister's sweat; at any time, as I've said, the situation could switch and did. We stood there and I tried as best I could to remember the details of Goran V. A younger man, perhaps thirty, with epilepsy. A sort of student—perhaps in theology? A habit of speech. What was it? He would begin to say one thing, decide against it, and then say something like the opposite, something safer than what he had been going to say. A dark person, Goran V. Lived alone in a small apartment in a former convent. He had sought it out because it was cheap and because he wanted to feel what nuns felt. Goran V was always framing things, always preparing things he would say to his doctoral advisor, a man named Ostriker. But they were never good enough. This was the role. Constance C, of course, I knew only through her performances. I did not see the Constance C dossier, nor any other dossier for my sister's characters. But Constance C was a victor, I knew that. She was always winning, visibly winning whatever was going on. She would charm everyone at every chance, but defeat them verbally too. In some way one had to speak to give Constance the chance of victory. This, Goran could easily do. Constance C had a boyfriend who was always rumored to be arriving, but never did. She would talk about him at length, tediously, if given the opportunity. Recalling all this, I went out into the house, and soon after, my sister followed. The hallway opens at that point into a large meeting room in which there are benches and a projector for watching films, which we rarely did, but loved to do. The benches of the room could be moved or hung on the walls to clear space, as for when we had some activity that required space. I believe this was a Shaker innovation, a kind of peg system run around the walls of the room in order to hang all things at need. Or so a teacher told me. Everything I knew about the world I knew through characters, through the dossiers. The information often conflicted. My mother as two different characters would disagree, would give us competing visions of the world and its peoples. My father would give still others. A dossier would specify that I should behave as if X were true, when that same day, inhabiting a different character, I would be forced to completely contradict that belief. I was not to think, so my parents said, that things were true per se. Things are true for people, for characters, for the costumes we wear. When we wear a different costume, a different thing is true. The world runs like water through your hands. I believe I sat for a moment on a bench by the wall because the light through the window at that hour passes the leaves of a tree, and I like to take another moment grasping my character before I am forced to speak. So I was sitting there and could hear, still in the hall, my sister crying softly. This struck me as strange, for I had never heard Constance C cry. My initial impulse, to ask her what had happened, was immediately stymied even as I took a step towards her. This was what hesitancy was, to hesitate even in the midst of hesitation. To not even know whether or how to stop hesitating, as if hesitating might or could be a thing in itself, rather than a nothing. I tried to imagine what James would say to a crying girl. He would comfort her, it must be. I should comfort her. So I went into the hall to do so, but she, noticing me, noticing that I had noticed her, was suddenly full of a kind of radiant Constance-like anger. She brushed past me harshly and was gone into the kitchen, winning somehow the interaction. I gulped and breathed hard. I was shaken by what had happened. Almost anything was too much for me. And already, anyway, I could hear them calling me into the kitchen. As I went I tried to know what it could mean for Goran to know what it might be for Constance to cry and how he would experience that visibly to the others. It was a puzzle. Usually I simply did what I felt, feeling as Goran V, but the bizarre gives rise to contradiction and confusion, and I was lost, which, luckily, was Goran V's natural element. Constance's boyfriend is arriving in a few minutes, my father told me, as I reached the kitchen. Clean yourself up. It is hard for me even to remember what it was I felt because now, not being Goran V, I have difficulty thinking as he thinks. If I were somehow to be back in that house, within that paradigm of stages, a host of feelings are accessible to me, and with them their attendant memories. But here I can only see the action as if from above, see myself, gesticulating in the kitchen, see my father pushing me towards the bathroom. For what reason does he want me to clean my face? Constance C's boyfriend is always arriving but never arrives. What hurry can there be? And equally, to the bathroom with great hurry, with complete understanding of why . . . In the past days, sitting here, I have often thought of my father and what his life must have been like before I, his son, met him. Of the many characters I saw him portray, there was one, Albert B, who I believe was based on his younger self, based on the man I never met. I think that my father took his younger self and placed it in a character that he would sometimes play for us. Or perhaps this is something I want to believe because Albert B was always so kind to me, kinder than any other. He would take me outside sometimes, more than anyone else did, would play with me, would touch me gently on the shoulder. My father almost never touched me as any of his characters, save in anger when I needed discipline, or for some medical purpose, or for grooming. But Albert B, of all his faces, Albert B would sit beside me, almost touching, and read to me from books, or tell me stories. He taught me to play chess and let me beat him. In no way did I ever have such joy or fondness from my mother, but I wonder: there was a character named Patricia J, one she often had when alone with my sister. It was a theory my sister told me, a theory about Patricia J and Albert B. Might they not simply be a kind of permission? That my parents give up the roles for a night and be themselves? Each had a dispensation, Patricia J for my sister, Albert B for myself? At some point Patricia J and Albert B did not come anymore, and there was no way we could ask for them, having ourselves no such language. Albert B told me a story once, a story about a theater. He said, speaking to me (I was in the role of another man, Chas, his junior, a sort of venal ladder-climber, yet not truly a bad person, just petty), he said, Chas, I know you think you know about theaters, but let me tell you, I used to work in a theater. Not like this dump. A real theater with multiple stages, hidden stages, stages beneath stages, rotating seat planes, slots to reach under the audience seats, the whole nine yards. We'd put on any play we liked. Whatever cast we picked, the best in the world would come just to use the stages, that's how great the place was. And what's more it was old, had always been that way. It wasn't some new technology. No, it was like a giant clock. The man who ran it, who showed me around there, he was a real stickler. I saw him beat someone with a stick for mispositioning a light. Sort of thing only happens once. Well, this guy took a liking to me, and gave me my start in theater. I was acting in a

play, some Ibsen imitation, and he said, no more acting for you. Now you are going to direct. The theater
is yours for the next open slot. I was overcome. I
know a bum like you couldn't guess what he would
do in a situation like that, but I knew more or less
how to handle it. I was a young guy, but I said, Well,
I do expect to get paid handsomely, and he started
laughing. In it for the money, are you? That was the
production I did with a nude audience. Just a typical
play, nothing special. The actors weren't even very
good, but the audience gets stripped naked by force
at the beginning of the play and kept there by hired
hooligans. At the end, we give them their clothes
back and let them go, but tell them there're plenty of
photographs which we'll release unless . . . if you take
my meaning. My father would, as Albert B, tell me
things like this, exposing a world of which I knew
nothing, and of which I could guess little, save that
he had left it for this impossible theater project that
had been settled on my head, on my head and on the
head of my sister. I suppose there were stories like
that Patricia told my sister, but I never heard them.
When we were small, not having roles yet, and we
would always play at the sullen/motile game, all day

every day the sullen/motile game, we would read books together in what I have come to understand is a rather strange way. We would get a children's book and sit in a circle. My father would read the whole book aloud, not showing us the images. Then the book would be passed to my sister, who would look at it awhile. Then she'd pass it to me, and I to my mother, who would put it away. If I took too long looking at the illustrations, my mother would say, You're done. I'm looking at the pictures, I would say, because I want to know ... There's nothing to know, she would say. The day is over. And we would go to bed. Then in bed, my sister would describe for me all the illustrations, even the ones I had seen. I loved to lie there listening. She would say, And on the first page there was a many-masted ship and all over it the pirate mice. And on the second page there was an island with ripples on it like the skin of an old dog, and in the folds were towns and all the windows of all the houses were lit up with candles. And on the third page, there was an owl, an old owl with a stocking cap. A what? A stocking cap, a wool hat that owls wear. He has spectacles too, and visitors. No one lives with him. But they seem to visit a lot. On she would go through the book, remembering. We had to be good rememberers—it was all our grace and all our delight. Sometimes I would sit there in the house, speaking to my mother, behaving as I was told, but in my skull I was remembering the leaves of the tree outside the window. I would remember each leaf I had seen, and count them, and when I was done, my mother would have turned away. Somehow whatever I must have said had been enough. I believe that in the course of my life my mother grew to hate me, and to hate my sister too. I do not say that because I have any knowledge of it really, nor because I observed her demonstrating the reality of hate to me in her person or intentions. But she somehow never strayed into gentleness. For nineteen years of my life, she never found any accidental gentleness to show me. Shouldn't she have done so by mistake at least once? There were many things that we hid from my parents. Of these, I can't say which they knew, and which were truly secret. I believe they must have known about our relations, but simply did not care. When we were younger we would steal sweets from the kitchen cabinet to eat in the night, and once when I was caught at this, my mother broke my arm. She said, Memory is an aid to learning. Will you please remember this? My father did not stop her. And you, she said to my sister, you, the one to whom he is bringing these sweets, know that the next thing will happen to you, if any next thing happens. But my sister was always calm. Which one would be caught doing which next thing, she asked, and for what? Greta? Joan? Constance? Maura? Who shall I be and how shall I be caught? To this my mother could say nothing. It was a mystery in some ways that my sister and I shared a room, as the house overall was rather large, and there certainly could have been space for another bedroom. I expect that it was simply part of the experiment, that we were thrown together in this way in order to form from us a single organism, bifurcated by day, joined by night. Discussions we would have, my sister and I, about what the experiment might be, and for how long it would go. Can it be, my sister would ask, that our parents intend to care for us our whole lives? And if not, if not, then what? Will we be released one day, like animals wandering out of broken enclosures at an abandoned farm, or a zoo in a bombed city?

The shape of the house seemed perhaps to imply that there had been a plan which they chose at some point not to act on. The house, or as much of it as we were allowed to enter, was a mirror. On one side, our bedroom and our line of tape, and on the other theirs, with an identical line (who knew what little rituals they had with each other—rituals of which we could know nothing). On one side, a narrow hallway and a living room, on the other, a narrow hallway and the kitchen. Their side had a closed bathroom, which was their privilege. Because we were not allowed any privacy, we were not allowed a bathroom. The toilet used by my sister and myself was in the open in the living room, there like any chair or couch. We had no shame about it, although we understood, from our study of characters, that others would. We never saw our parents use this toilet, although perhaps it was at times used as a prop in one or another humorous way. Though the humor may be hard to find. There is little room for the vulgar or the grotesque in a life that is completely public. There was another building, too, just beyond a short lawn the other side of their bedroom. We never went there, and I never saw them go either, but we wondered, as anyone would, what it contained. Did it contain some next thing, some next element or development? In the end, we decided that, like everything else beyond the house, it might as well be imaginary, had no bearing, could not touch us, was not, in any way, to be hoped for, looked for, dreamt of.

Perhaps they sensed in us this fatalism. My mother or father, alternately, would promise us that we would go on a trip. This was a kind of narrative game with them. Who wants to go on a trip? my mother would say. Or my father would sit down on the couch beside me and clap his hands to his legs and say, Well, kid, where should we go? knowing full well that we would go nowhere, that in fact, we never had gone anywhere, and that there was no intention whatsoever for us to go. I suppose it must have been a shared thing between them, a kind of pleasure they could be afforded to mock us for the smallness of our experience, the never-going-anywhere of our psyches in their encountering physical space. The limitations were brushed up against worse those few times we watched films. Ah, my father would say, how fine it is to be in a forest, or to swim in a lake, as the hero plunged alternately through underbrush or through a watery swell. Even to see a horse (which I had never seen) running with other horses was almost too much for my sister and me. I believe we fainted together, fainted at once as a pair, when I was thirteen and they showed us a frog being eaten by a snake. I don't know what they meant by it, but my mother took notes and my father peered at us, his chair turned away from the flickering light.

My sister and I would sit sometimes in the bedroom simply saying words out loud, names of things, as if for no reason, simply to hear the sound of each other's voice. Let us name animals, for twenty seconds, she would say. Go! Rock dove. Dolphin. Antelope. Frilled lizard. Grizzly bear. Leopard. Jackal. Monitor. Kinkajou. Good! Gull. Rat. Monkey. Bat. Onager. Sea eagle. Porcupine. Stop.

But this last-day birthday was not like any other, for it was a day to contain other days, recursive like a box. We had been waiting for it some time. I have been thinking of something, my sister said to me. I want to tell you but I am afraid that you will not want to hear it. Who should I be to hear it? I asked her. Be Geddes, he listens well. I will be, she hesitated, I will be Inez, and I am, she faltered a little, still afraid you will not agree. I agree, I told her, when have I not agreed to anything you asked. Not once, she said, not once, but this would be the once. Do you remember, she began, faltering. Do you remember, she said, herself then visibly remembering, being moved by the thing she said, when you had a fever three years ago this winter? I don't remember much, I said. I was in a bad way. Well, I remember it all. It got cold suddenly. It was some kind of gentle autumn and then, suddenly, we were dropped in the depths of winter. All the windows were shut for the season. As mother says, I am shutting the windows for the season, or, Come help me shut the windows for the season. We will put windows on the windows. Then we get to go outside for once, helping her put the windows on the windows in some great effort to block the cold. Whether it was true or not, Mother and Father traced your fever to that day, for you were out longer than you should have been in the cold, and that night you began to rant and sweat feebly out of every inch of your body. You couldn't speak to us. Father and Mother kept you on the living room floor in a swaddle of blankets and for three days we thought you would die. This thing, this thinking you would die was one of the strangest things I have seen in my life. It appears to have been felt not at all by our parents, who simply sat and waited and took notes. Occasionally they would bring you water or a cold cloth. No one patted you even once or held your hand or made any gesture consistent with that of a person who wished for your recovery. One could almost say they seemed bored by the situation, desperate for it to resolve itself one way or the other. In fact, they paid no attention to me. It was as if, looking at you lying senseless on that pallet, they were looking through a telescope at your eventual death, and desiring it, but doing nothing to bring it closer. It was with a disturbing patience that they oversaw your sickness. And all the while, in a mortal terror, I circled the periphery, not even remembering who I was to be or what I was to say. It was at that time, at the moment when your fever broke, that I realized what it is that we should do and how it is that we can do it. What do you mean? I asked. Put your hands here, she said. I put them where she said, on the scars beneath my arms, and she, she reached to mine. This was a habit of hers when she would say something she meant, something that felt to her, as she said, like a thing dropped down a well. She said to me then, I have a plan, the plan that burst up in me the day your fever broke. She, Inez, she said, pressing her forehead to mine, boring into me with eyes I could not focus on, eyes that could not possibly focus on me, What if, she said, what if when I am twenty-one we begin a two-year, a two-year . . . procedure? What would the procedure be? It would be the end, the end of the experiment, this thing we're in. The subjects of the experiment would choose for the experiment to end. On my birthday, you would help me, we would kill myself. We would do it together in a delicate and elaborate procedure, one we would spend our time planning this whole next year. We would kill me, that's what I'm saying, together we would kill me. But I am nearly two years older than you, so to make things even for the two years I waited for you, two long years you must remember, during which I did not even know you existed, an awful time, to be sure, you would then wait one year, eleven months, three days and kill yourself, taking care to follow the identical procedure and ceremony as we will use for this girl that you know, me. What do you say? At the time of our plan, I was eighteen and she twenty. She stood in the light practically glittering. I spun and flew in my body but had no breath to speak. It is a real, a real . . . I said finally, clutching her to me; we agreed to let nothing stop us. We were decided. It seemed inevitable suddenly, something we had not known, but that immediately we felt we had always known. How else could it have gone? Where there had been some indistinct thing growing year by year in our hearts, now there was nothing but certainty, and in that certainty an indisputable and incontestable joy, not abstract, but joy in the limbs. One could leap and did, knowing the extreme limit of this life. So we had chosen our way.

Sometimes in dreams, I was taken to places I never went. We watched films and what I saw there gave me places to go, and when I went there I wondered what else there would be for me. Waking, I was never sure I couldn't be at some time in the future, somewhere else, something different, entirely different from what I was and knew. Many people are persuaded by reality. I was persuaded by my dreams, but not ever to become who they promised me. Rather to know and feel the weight of what I had lost, even before I had lost it. I made the meaning of my life from the things that were denied me, by experiencing the delight of them in my imagination. My sister showed me this, how to do this, and we did it together. It was a roundabout sort of rebellion, invisible to the naked eye. When we spoke about our deaths, about this operation we would employ to conclude this grand experiment, when she went from me then and stepped away across the room to perform some small task there was space there between us, and the bed there, and I dove to her across the space in sudden mortal terror, as if, suddenly, no time could be wasted. Our whole lives suddenly seemed such profligate use of the energy given us, of our so-specified motility, and in my fear I wanted everything of her at every moment. She had moved but inches, and I caught her to me and we collapsed into each other and onto the hard bed and then down to the floor to lie in a kind of pile as some species of impossible shiny gladness, something no one must have ever seen. I have certainly never seen it. One can only be it. There is no appearance to such joy. In the days, my sister said to me, as quietly as I have ever heard her speak, we will do as we have always done, and be the way we have been, but more so, more gently, with great persistence and patience. In the nights we will occupy ourselves with each other, with this love, and with our glorious deaths. Can we be so happy? I asked her. Anyone can choose this, she said. Anyone.

That light that lights the way for me is dimmed not at all by the beginning that we made. That this collision and that collision have landed me here, in a strange place I do not recognize, as a roleless person I do not even myself know, is something we thought might well happen. Once she would die, we expected it was a matter of dice. Most likely was that my parents would kill me immediately. I thought that and so did she. But they did not kill me. They arranged for police to come and take me away, and they made statements about my behavior, seeing to it I would not return. I did not expect any kindness from them, as it would have been the first real kindness they had ever given me, and one never expects to receive anything for the first time, or shouldn't. From the moment of my sister's death, I felt I was afloat in a power not my own, as part of a procedure I myself had adopted, an intricate ending for a joined life of which I could not have been more fond. My sister's death was my death, was the beginning of my death. I sit here as a person, but am not a person in any real sense. I am taking the eager steps to death, though my feet stand still.

These past days I have sometimes wondered if our suicides were not planned, if, before my parents ever gave birth to us, they, in their description of the experiment they were to make, did not specify there on the paper that our most likely death would be at our own hands, that this was the obvious way in which the experiment would conclude. Thinking this, I imagine that they must have been surprised, year after year, when we did not kill ourselves, and that perhaps this was the reason the punishments mounted as time passed. Perhaps they were egging us on to our deaths. Whatever disbelief then was in my mother's eyes, each day as she greeted us, was not suspicion over whether we were properly playing our parts, but rather the incredulous picture of skepticism: How could these two yet manage day by day to continue before our very eyes as if they are living a life when we know very well they have none? This was the question she must have asked herself. Perhaps they did not know how much of a life we had, so well we had hidden it. Of course this interpretation is contrary to the often stated utopian hopes my parents had laid out so often, hopes that they, in us, could make two people who might function independent of so many snaring threads of identity and odious culture. If they did believe truly that they could make us such forthright non-people, through the operations of constant theater (as it were), it could not have been with a mind to us living real lives as non-people, for among whom would such non-people live? How could they make their way? It seems more likely the whole thing was more elemental than that: it was the playing-out of curiosity and the collision of cynicism and bleakness. In simplest form: something had to fill my parents' lives; a kind of game at our expense would do the job. The questions my sister and I had asked ourselves the entire duration of our childhood vis-à-vis our parents' intentions were questions without answers, for they had no intentions following the cessation of our childhood. Our parents did not mean for us to survive childhood. When I say it like this, it seems certain to me. In any case, survive childhood we did not, I and my glorious sister. We came to its edge, there to lie down. But this lying down, such an empty and light, such a small thing. I think of the birthday celebration in the house, which, at the time, my sister and I, we thought we were the only ones celebrating our deaths, that this was some secret, but now I must suppose that my parents, expecting our deaths, passed each birthday celebration with the promise that there would not be another. In effect, therefore, though we did not know it, we were all celebrating the same thing.

My sister sat at the head of the table. She was in the role of Gemma H, a rather loud and boisterous woman, a nurse, twice divorced, with children she no longer knew. I was Jonny P, a child violinist who is never given credit for any inner life, but on whom others pin their dreams. My mother was a woman we called Aunty, a sort of hybrid family member and antagonist of some other class, always bringing critical opinions about the way we do things, or telling exemplary tales that prove our habits ill-considered. My father was some version of first teacher, who now more and more seemed retired. More and more perhaps it seemed he had said everything he knew out loud on any number of occasions. The kitchen where we sat was a wide square room with a steel sink, a large stove, and a metal table such as you would find in a lab or commercial kitchen. That was on one side, the cooking side, along with a wall of spices, beans, grains, etc. On the other side there was a wooden table at which supper was eaten with two benches and a chair at either end. It was not so big that you could not lean towards someone meaningfully, but large enough to take whatever various dishes would make a supper. There were windows running down both sides of the room. On one side they looked away down the black hill towards a swampy wood into which we had been forbidden ever to go, and into which we never did go. On the other they peered into a hallway that would permit one to pass the kitchen without entering it, though I don't know why anyone would find it useful to do so. My parents had hung a series of lithographs along the hall. At one point, educationally, the lithographs would be altered in keeping with our studies. No longer. The same set had been up for a number of years. They were illustrations of various archaeological digs, evidently taken from old magazines made prior to the consummate use of photography. One could see the various workers scrabbling around the sites, which invariably looked rather august and grand. There everything was cleaner than in real life. I mention these only because, sitting there in the kitchen, I often looked through the little windows or saw the lithographs out of the corner of my eye. Somehow their existence seemed to me contrary to the general principles of my parents' life, and therefore a kind of glimpse of a weakness that had always existed, even before the struggle began, a weakness that perhaps made inevitable the failure of the entire design. That is to say: if my father and mother longed for a time when it seemed that the answers to the present would be found in the past, and worse, that the answers to the present would be found in a nostalgic colonial past, and if in that feeling they put upon the wall of our house emblems of that ridiculous belief, then it seems obvious they would themselves never have the strength to confront the essential nature of day-to-day life in all its empty viciousness. My sister was speaking, that is, Gemma H was speaking to Aunty. She said, I was at the Rasmussens' last week and they told me a remarkable story. Perhaps you would like to hear it. By all means, my father said. We would all like to be entertained by your little story, I am sure. Then in that case, I will tell it, continued Gemma. The Rasmussens, as you know, breed dogs, and not just dogs, but a very specific kind of dog. They breed dogs which they sell to the labor enforcement division. Now you know that the labor enforcement division is tasked with ensuring that there is a constant supply of all foodstuffs, and must see to it that the workers who live on the group farms do what they are supposed to do and work. And of course the workers are always attempting to run off one way or another, or sit under a tree, or do something else, anything really, other than work, and so the dogs have to be trained to tell the difference between the two types of people you would find on a group farm: the labor heavies and the workers. So it's a puzzle. Do you know how they do it? She looked at my mother, my father, and me, turning her face one way then another. I don't know, I said. It was a thing Jonny P often found it possible to say. Do you know? I asked my father. He had to confess he didn't know either. They do it by scent, said Gemma H. But not any scent that the workers or the labor division thugs naturally produce. Instead, the labor division gives their employees a kind of chemical that makes their glands emit a particular scent. That scent allows them to go back and forth across the areas around the farm, the areas where the dogs are. But if you don't have that proper smell and you go there, well . . . you can imagine what happens. Old Rasmussen showed me a few of the dogs, really big dogs, about the size of donkeys. They were friendly, but by god I'd hate to meet one out in the open. Just to see it coming after me . . . I'd fold right up, let alone six or eight of them. As she finished her story my father had brought out the food we were to eat. He put the dishes variously around the table, and laid out silverware. I thought to myself, This is the last meal my sister will eat, and I peered at her as she looked at a dish of green beans that sat in front of her on the table. A dish of green beans, something she had eaten hundreds of times, was now final. All that it had about it, its preparation, its geometry, the traditions it set forth by its very being, the memories of all the previous dishes of green beans, they rotated in the air about this green bean dish and she reached down through it and took some and put them on her plate. I wonder, I said to myself: Will she eat at all? Or merely look at each thing, choose a thing, choose another thing? I thought, too, whatever she does, it will be something like this you try to do, later, when your turn comes. I wanted nothing more than to match her. She said then to my parents, I ate on the way, so I'm not very hungry. But I will eat a green bean. And she put one on her fork and raised it to her lips. No one will make you eat more than you want to, my father said, but we have other things here on the table. I took the plate of green beans, took some from it, and ate one, just as my sister was eating hers. She did not look at me as I did this, nor did she seem to care at all about anything I did. Gemma H despised Jonny, disliked music in general, and children. She was known to never address comments his way. It seemed to me a kind of punishment my parents were inflicting on us for continuing to live that we should on this birthday not be permitted to truly interact with each other. It was the sort of thing my mother must have thought of—or the thing I would imagine her thinking of, whether she was capable of doing it or not. I would not want to have my gland emitting any extra smell, I said. Would you? My mother said that she had in the entirety of her life attempted to avoid emitting unnecessary smells, to which my father added that the group-farm-dog-avoiding-smell could hardly be called unnecessary. Gemma H voiced her agreement, and mentioned again that the dogs she had seen were just about the size of donkeys. She did this in an extremely tiresome manner which I found delightful. Still I could see in her some stiffness, like she was elsewhere, preparing. She launched into the next speech, half rising to her feet and mimicking the greater girth she imagined Gemma H to have. The Rasmussens' daughter, she continued, that pompous little bitch, has a boyfriend named Hank, quite a tall fellow, looks like a hawk or some kind of predator cat. I'd met him before once or twice. While I was there, I was on my way to use the bathroom and do you know what I saw? The door to Chrissy's bedroom was open and I saw she had got down on all fours on the floor and let Hank climb on top of her. She had her hands all tangled up in the carpeting. It was all white and furry like someone's hair, and her hands were tangled up in it like she couldn't think of anything to do with them but grab the floor. She was just there on the ground letting anything at all happen to her however it would. Why, I just about opened my mouth wide and screamed. Don't believe I've ever seen the like. But you know, what I really did, well, I stopped there in the hall and watched them, you know they are both rather well-made people, and just as I was standing there, Chrissy's eyes met mine, I mean, she looked up at me there where I stood and . . . That moment my mother grabbed my sister, somehow she had come up behind her and she grabbed her and forced her to the floor. My father brought the training aid and applied it to my sister's arm, and she shrieked and shook and tried to get away. But they shocked her again and she lay looking stupidly up at them with no expression at all on her face. Every time this year, my father said, the same lessons need to get taught. Out of character. You'd think it would become clear what a person would and wouldn't say, he said, shaking his head. Why don't you go lie down. Jonny P, help Gemma to the back of the house. Supper is over. I came around and helped her to her feet. I could feel her arm as I took it: the arm was deadly cold, completely cold, having no warmth whatsoever. I suppose it was that she had been lying on the cold floor, but it somehow gave me the immediate presentiment of her death, as if she had already begun it. I stumbled, and caught myself, and helped her from the kitchen.

Back in our room there was still some light, for our little window was west. My sister sat down on the floor and I sat beside her. Just like I said, she said, just like I said I'd do. I'd make them go after me one last time, for kicks, just to remember who they are. Do you remember? I asked. Oh, I remember, she said. We looked at each other and looked. It wasn't necessary to smile or show anything at all. Such things weren't necessary. Did you get the pills? I told her that I had gone to our parents' bathroom, that I had gotten the pills. And there they were, a plastic jar full of pills, enough pills for whatever anyone wanted such pills for. They are faun-colored, she said, and they were. The pills were a sort of pinkish-gray color there on her hand. It made my stomach clench to see them there in her hand. Not yet, I said. Don't tell me not yet. I know the way it will go. She put the pills on the windowsill and leaned against the wall. Suddenly the wall seemed dirty and fond. I could see it as if up close, see it as I never could see the wall before. I was fond of it, felt its rarity. It was the wall that was near us then. I'm afraid, she said. The end feels very close. It is close, I told her, I can feel it too. I'm afraid too. You can't be afraid, she said. Or I can't be. One of us knows how to do this without being afraid. One of us must. I lay on my side and looked at her. The room was now dark. I felt I shouldn't be the one to put the light on, not unless she wanted me to, but I didn't want to ask. I did it, I put a little lamp on. Shall we go by the plan, I said. Let's go by the plan, she said. We had argued so many nights, late into the night, and argued so many mornings, lying in the dawn, whispering and whispering and whispering: How would the thing be done? What was it, the ceremony we would make? What was the best way, if there was a best way? There must be a best way, my sister said, a best way for us. Should I die while we fuck? Should I be dying as you make love to me? Or would that make you feel bad? She couldn't decide, would that be good for her but bad for me, or good for me but bad for her. What do you think? I said I would do whatever she wanted, but I didn't know if I could. Maybe the time would come to do it and I could not. Something like that is hard to know. I might be in a strange state of mind. Perhaps that part we can't plan, she said. She said, What about the listing game? I said, What about it? She said maybe that's the way. Maybe we play the listing game, and as we do it the pills take effect. You said you read the instructions on the bottle. I read them, I said. You get drowsy and drowsier and then you're out. I don't know how long it takes. Could be if you take a lot it goes quicker. I don't know. She always scratched at her arm where they would shock her, a kind of grayish place, a matted area of skin like somewhere a deer lies down, she scratched at it absently. I have to take enough, she'd said. That can't be the mistake we make. So over time we came to our conclusions. We decided she would ruin the supper and get us sent away. We decided we would sit and wait for it to get dark. We decided we would talk for a while, talk and maybe touch our hands. Then at some point it was up to me. I would stand and go to get a drink of water. When I brought back the water, she would drink it and with it she would swallow the pills. Then we would lie on the bed, staring up, and we would play the listing game. We would play it, and at some point I would say something and she would say nothing. That was the plan.

We were concerned, though, that when it was my turn to do the same thing it wouldn't work the way we wanted it to, because I couldn't do it by myself the way we had done it together. It was important to us that we do it the same way twice if we could. What if we use a camera, I said, what if we film it? Then I could have the film and use it later. In the first place, we have no camera. In the second place, there's no guarantee that you will be able to keep anything

or have anything in the future. Once I am dead, you
don't know what they'll do to you, where you'll go or
be kept. It will be a hard thing even for you to get the
pills you'll need to use. I thought of that, I said. Half
of these I'll sew into the sleeve of my shirt. Then all
I have to do is hold on to this shirt. Maybe she said.
But I doubt you'll keep the camera. It has to be—it
has to be that you memorize everything we say. You
have to memorize it exactly, and when it is your turn,
you have to say the whole thing out, just the way
we said it. You have to say it all to yourself, wherever you are. I'll begin it, we'll be in it together now,
and then when you do it, it will be the same: we'll be
in it together then. Just to talk about it was awful.
But the awfulness was somehow bright, bright like
cheerfulness. It made us feel something. The nothing that we had begun to feel at all times over the
deadening course of our lives was penetrated by the
promise of our deaths, and made light and cheerful.
Suddenly we had something to look forward to. That
something was: the few things left before we would
die, our preparations and the exquisite attention we
could pay to them. Through it all, we sat there, in
our small room, shoulders pushing into one another,

arms, legs entangled. I smelled her and felt anxiety like a great wave: this was something I would no longer smell. I want to keep something from you, I said, so I can smell it when I take the pills. They will take it from you, she said. You have to remember the smell.

We were there in the little light of the lamp and she held my one hand in both of hers. She sat there with the broken posture of a child, leaning half-forward over my arm. I was leaned forward too, and in this way my cheek touched her ear. There was no sound whatsoever in the house, just an occasional creaking or noise of wind against the window. Should we talk, I said. We thought maybe we would talk about something at this point. I don't know, she said. I was thinking of something to say, but you know it already. I mean, I said it to you already. I was thinking of the things that will happen to you when they find me. Let's not think of that, I said. Why? she asked. Because it isn't interesting. If we face each other what is interesting is between us. The things that are behind our backs, that circle out there, they are beneath our notice, and what will happen to me when you are gone is simply beneath notice. It can be anything and it will be the same. It will be the same, she said, and she tried to kiss me, but our mouths were too strange to do it properly. I felt I could vomit, but it was as if my stomach weren't connected to my throat. I had nowhere to vomit from or to. It was just my body erupting against some invisible edge that we kept brushing up against. We could hardly speak then, but gave each other what there was by leaning, just leaning. I felt the floor then through my legs and wished it were harder. The moment went and went, we could hardly bear it, and what happened then was awful, what happened then was that I found that I was returning with a glass of water. I had already gone and gotten it. I could remember standing, remember letting go of her hands, remember her looking up at me as I stood. How could I have missed it happening while it happened? And now I was returning, standing there before her, kneeling, offering her the water, offering her the pills. So little could I be myself that this, the principal event of my life, could pass as if it had happened to someone else. She took the water, she took the pills, she swallowed them. We stood, uncertainly, and went to the bed. There was already in her some opacity, something through which I could not see the way I always had. It is this thing I will have too, I thought, but I will have it alone. There where she lay on the bed, she had put herself down no way I knew. I knew every way she could lie on a bed, every way she had, but somehow I had never seen it this way. I wanted to know how I could lie beside her, but suddenly didn't know how to begin. Then a fear came that she was already gone, and I was there beside her, and looking up, and her hand was in mine, and she squeezed it. She squeezed my hand. She was still there.

I will begin, she said. You were standing by the front door and you were maybe three. You knew you were to sit down, but you wouldn't. Mother was holding a watering can, and she dropped it. That's how much she wanted to get to the training aid. She ran and got it and came back and you were still not sitting. I think she was afraid you would sit in the meantime. Then she held you down with one arm and did you with the other. I don't remember that, I said. You were speaking lines of Hector D, last year. Father wasn't really listening. You began to say things that weren't right. He didn't hear you and so you went on and on, making it clearer and clearer. Finally you started to shout. You just started to shout things at him, things you thought, and the two of them, they set upon you, dragged you down and did it. You were in convulsions for two days. You wouldn't come out of your room, I said. I think you were about ten. I was outside waiting on the tape line, and you were in bed and you wouldn't come. They called to you and called to you. Finally, they went in there, and shocked you where you lay. That's the only time it happened in here. In here, she said. I had forgotten about that. Somehow I felt that nothing bad had ever happened in here.

You were doing a drawing with Mother. She was being a grandmother, I think, some grandmother, she hasn't done that one in years. You were, you were the one they got rid of that time during the storm. They got rid of her because ... Gladys O, she said. That's right, Gladys O. You were drawing on a piece of cardboard, and she started telling you what you should draw, and you drew it, you drew the thing she said to draw, and she hit you. I remember she hauled off and hit you and then you were just drooling, just on your face on the carpet and drool came out of your mouth. I was only six or seven. I just stood there and did nothing.

———

You, she said, you there, hold on to me. This is our joy, she said, this person who at that time could speak and be heard by me. There she was, still speaking, and I, there, still hearing. I reached and held on to her, saying also, This is our joy, saying it with my mouth stiff like cardboard, I turned, and held on to her and with her leg she wreathed me, and I ran my hand along her head, over her head, which was shaved short just like mine, which was always just like mine, this person who always had been just like me, even before I was, and pressed the side of my head against hers, our ears against each other's. I am finding you here, she said. What do you mean? I am finding you, she repeated, but slower. I don't, I . . . She was shaking a little, and her breath was shallow. I could feel her less and less. She was less and less. Please, I cried, say something. Say something. When I saw you coming, she said, you had the water in your hand. You were bringing it to me. You brought it to me. You . . . How was this supposed to go? Are we doing it right? We are doing it right, I said. She sighed and turned into me. She turned into me.

No one can know what my father or mother felt, coming into that room the next day and seeing what had happened. Our opinion, my sister's and mine, was that the body of my sister, her dead body, that cadaver, the thing she had always been (a thing concealed by her life), would in no way shock them. In fact, they were waiting for this next transition. They were perhaps desperate for their experiment to conclude, to fail, so they could go on to whatever was next. Who knows what sort of thing is or would be next for them? Who knows even where they are now? They saw the body of my sister there in its inimitable wreck. They saw me, sitting by it, had known, I am sure, that I would be there sitting by a corpse, or knew the opposite: they would find my sister sitting by my body, my corpse, my glorious cadaver. Whichever was left they would discard. I am sure it scarcely mattered. They did not cry out. Perhaps they had total certainty the moment neither of us stood at the tape line when we ought to have been standing. The tape line was a thing we had mastered, a thing we knew so well. Wake up, stand at the tape line. Be told who to be and how. When we were not there, and when time passed, and they knocked on the door and we were not there at the tape line, the line they evidently enjoyed the use of with such extreme consistency, it must be true: this deviation gave total knowledge. Either I or my sister was now a corpse and the thing was over. The proof of it came next. The door opened. I looked up. My father and mother were there, looking into that tiny room. It was perhaps seven feet by five feet. There was faint day then, enough to see. The wooden board of the bed took up half the room, which now anyone could tell was a very shabby place, scarcely the setting for all of life's joy. I was on the floor next to the bed, and my sister, who I had pulled to the ground, was partly underneath, with her useless head in my lap. I was leaned against a small radiator and above it was the window that had given us so much light, the indefatigable window. Whatever we asked of it, it had given us. My parents were looking down at me from the door and I up at them. I could feel their total commitment in something about which I knew nothing.

Their participation in my life had been entirely clean, as clean as the inside of a stone. Our eyes met, but somehow could not meet, for they were looking at me as at something inanimate, as something that could never be the origin of meaning or judgment. They saw me as what I was, disposable, beyond pathetic, an object that had played its part. They shut the door and I could hear from the living room my father on the telephone, a thing that had never happened in all the days of our life together. So easily he did it, he used the telephone and called for someone to come and take me away.

When I think of the body that lay in my lap, it stirs. In memory it cannot stay so still, for her death was for me a brief thing: some seven hours in a room, one lidless night; but her life was longer, was what I know, what we had promised for ourselves. And so the body becomes animate again. The mouth stirs, trembles. The eyes open. My sister is alive in my arms. The door to the room is shut. Some constant light, constant light of a never-dawned day is all around. The silence of the house is patient, comforting: we may fill it with whatever we like. No one now will ever come to disturb us. No one can. She raises herself, ever so slightly, sees me, smiles. Her tongue comes out the corner of her mouth, licks her dry lips wet once more, and she is in my arms and our embrace is the contract of the death I am already so ready for, the death I go to. Oh, my sister, can it be that anyone has ever been so happy?

ACKNOWLEDGMENTS

Thanks to:

Jim Rutman, Kendall Storey and all at Catapult, the city of New Orleans, where I began part 1, and Café Marie-Jeanne at the corner of California and August in Humboldt Park (since shuttered), where I wrote the record of the black hill.

© Lin Woldendorp

JESSE BALL is an absurdist whose prizewinning work has been translated into more than twenty languages. He is on the faculty at the University of Virginia, where he is the Sydney Blair Memorial Professor of Creative Writing.